❑❑❑❑❑

Cimbri tugged on Whit's arm and steered them down a side street--or what was left of a side street. The firestorm that had swept through Isis had left mostly rubble. A few house shells stood, blackened hulks of stone that lined the weed-grown roads like silent sentinels of grief.

Suddenly she stopped, certain Whit would not resist her. She pulled the hard, muscled body against her, caught Whit's head and brought it down, within reach of a searching tongue. Whit shook in her arms, the fierce blast of response pouring helplessly from her, the white-hot desire Cimbri remembered.

Angry, Whit thrust her away. "Stop It!"

Cimbri wanted her so badly then that even this vast graveyard was not going to deter her. She placed her hands on Whit's shoulders and pushed her back against the scorched rock of a napalmed house. Gripping the thick, dark hair, Cimbri brought her lips to just below Whit's and stayed there, waiting. They were so close they were breathing into each other's mouths.

Return to Isis

Return to Isis

Isis

Jean Stewart

RISING TIDE PRESS

5 KIVY ST.,
HUNTINGTON STATION,
N.Y. 11746

Rising Tide Press
5 Kivy Street
Huntington Station, NY 11746
(516) 427-1289

Printed in the United States on acid-free paper

Publisher's note:
All characters, places and situations in this book are fictitious and any
resemblance to persons (living or dead) is purely coincidental.

Publisher's Acknowledgments:
The publisher is grateful for all the support and expertise offered by
the members of its editorial board: Bobbi Bauer, Adriane Balaban,
Beth Heyn, Harriet Edwards and Pat G. And a special thanks to
Harriet and Adriane for their excellent proofing and criticism, to Edna
G. for believing in us, and to the feminist bookstores for being there.

First printing July, 1992
10 9 8 7 6 5 4 3 2

Edited by Lee Boojamra and Alice Frier
Book cover art: Evelyn Rysdyk

Library of Congress Cataloging-in-Publication Data
Stewart, Jean, 1953—
        Return to Isis/ Jean Stewart
            p.cm

ISBN 0-9628938-6-2   92-060175
                                       CIP

For my Susie

Artemis
Isis
Boudica
The Wilderness
Whit's Railroad Route
Free Land
Harvey
Toxic Zone
Old Vegas
Morgan
Susan B.
Tubman
Lang
Baubo's Farm
Chicago
Bethesda
Elysium
Atlantic ocean
Gulf of Mexico

— 1 —

"A woman," the burly trooper sneered.

"She ought to be breeding, not going around acting like a man," the other one grunted in agreement.

They gave her the once-over, their eyes lingering boldly on her breasts and crotch.

She kept her eyes down, as required, hating this demeaning ritual.

They were Regulators and she was a Computer Technician, both of equal rank in the rigid caste system of Elysium. The Regs were the police brawn that bullied a decaying society into order, while the Computer Techs maintained the machine intelligence network that provided the brains. For a Computer Tech to be also female was an anomaly, but these two had seen her and her tool box in this government building many times before. They knew her story and so tolerated her.

Two years ago, she was the beggar who had hustled a meal by repairing the Procurator's car, which had died in the street. The man had been late for an appointment with a superior, when she had passed by. Looking over the shoulder of the harassed Computer Tech, she modestly suggested that he vacuum the road dust from the unit. An educated guess which impressed the official. The Procurator had been ecstatic when his sleek, electric car started. He had called her 'his Idiot Savant' and put her on his staff.

The Regs knew the oft-repeated story, but they still made a big production out of checking her identification pass, her caste bracelet. Dumping the contents of her tool box and searching for concealed weapons also seemed to give them some perverse pleasure.

Even in her carefully hidden annoyance she was patient, since she knew this charade of who-was-in-charge would end soon. The Equipment Preservation Program was top priority. After all, the Procurator himself had sent for her to accomplish this difficult task.

The Elysian rulers didn't like the fact that a woman was so gifted at overhauling the ancient CD ROM units. However, when they had need of a repair, they called her. And they always made her pay for the way they needed her, for the way they had to set aside their asinine rules on gender-function.

"She's too hard-looking for me. Look at her—built like a damn serf." The large, intimidating Reg reached to his pants and casually re-adjusted his balls. Whit wasn't sure if he was showing her or himself that he had them.

The smaller of the two Regs squeezed her right biceps, while oh so accidentally brushing her breast in the process. She quickly decided that this weasel-faced man was the more dangerous of the two policemen.

Whit knew there were special rules from the Procurator, protecting women such as herself, women with necessary talents, from the routine gropes and even forced sexual acts most Elysian women endured. But the way this Regulator's eyes strayed over her told her that he regularly broke those rules.

"She's gotta work out to be like this," the Reg commented.

He was right, she did work out, exercising for hours alone in her tiny room, trying to blast away the deadly lack of humanity she lived with each day.

There was no honest consolation in Elysium. Heartfelt confidences were routinely for sale. Friendships were officially discouraged as "sentimental and frivolous." Whit talked to no one, nor had she read a book, heard a musical instrument, or contemplated a painting, in two years. She had long since been ground down by the hateful narrow-mindedness of this place. Exercising to exhaustion seemed to be the only way she could cope. And if the strong muscles were repulsive to these oafs, then she would get even stronger.

"Why aren't you working yet, lazy Cunt?" the weasel-faced, little man barked.

That was her permission to get started on her task.

Quickly, Whit moved past them to the empty office area. She took a screwdriver from her tool kit and began disassembling the housing on the computer. From the corner of her eye she watched the large Reg leave, while the smaller one set up a chair at the entrance to the room. She became engrossed in systematically checking the archaic machine. Within minutes, she had found the loose card, and tightened the right screw. The computer was operational again.

And now she could accomplish the actual purpose of her work in Elysium.

Whit rapidly typed in her password, switching all keyboard functions to the hidden micro molecular electronic device she had installed in this computer during the first repair, months ago. The Decency Scanner, which policed all computer usage in Elysium, would continue to read the test program running on the standard, almost ridiculously simple CD ROM. She would be safe for several moments, safe to at last link up with the satellite suspended in space over a century ago.

This particular computer, the Procurator's own, was on-line with the Regulation Bureau main frame, where the police files were stored. Every piece of information the police had was stored in those files. And she had serendipitously guessed the access code— Stud #1, the nickname imprinted on the vanity plates of the Procurator's beautiful Corvette, a leftover relic that had been rendered functional. It had been an easy guess, really. She had discovered that most of these men had computer access codes which involved some exaggerated description of their cocks.

After two years of subservience, her moment had finally come. She knew the code she needed to use, she was working on the machine that could link with the main frame itself. Two years of undercover effort was coming to a head.

She glanced at the door and saw the Regulator lovingly wipe a polishing cloth over his ceremonial Roman sword. Sweet Mother, how they loved all things Roman. They chose to think of themselves as the second Roman Empire. Whit found it laughable. What they actually were was a bad imitation of the Third Reich.

She knew this Reg had been given the sword in recognition of merit a few weeks back. Merit. The capture of three disease-free girls in the market place. It was rumored that there had been four, but that the Reg had raped and then killed the young woman, really a child, before delivering the others.

Whit shuddered and entered the password. In another second she was into the sealed security files, the complete, detailed operations of the Elysium Regulators. Copying the data she needed, she sent it to the weathered satellite dish on the rooftop. Last week, she had wheedled permission to go up there, claiming the external ventilator filters were awry and causing dust problems in the building's computers. In reality, she had been readying the old satellite dish for this transmission. Whit typed in the last command, and then the uploaded data went zipping through long unused wiring to the satellite dish. If all was going according to her plan, the stream of information was bouncing off its target, an abandoned NASA satellite, and then shooting back down to earth, to Lilith's computer in Freeland.

For a century now, the old NASA satellites had been spinning in space, their capacities largely unknown to the descendants of the people who had placed them there. Just another sad paradox of the Second Dark Ages.

So much had been lost in 2010, when America had embraced order over reason. Even now, in the year 2093, the two countries that had emerged from the Great Schism continued to move in completely opposite directions.

4

In moments, the transmission was over. She checked on the green-jacketed Reg. He seemed to have found a stubborn smudge and was very focused on removing it. Whit decided she had time for a precursory safe-check.

She opened the most recent Arrest File. Her eyes moved quickly over the usual long list, until they snagged on her cover name. She read quickly, as her heart squeezed tight with fear:

COMPUTER TECH WHIT HASTINGS, Bureau 4317, Office Park 902, Bethesda, Maryland: Freeland warrior, disease-free. TAKE ALIVE/RAPE OPTIONAL.

Whit looked at the Reg across the room and swallowed hard. She switched the machine from the molecular electronic device, or MED mode, to normal Teledex 586 system, and then removed the MED. The Reg guided the sword into the short leather scabbard he wore around his waist. She had to do something, before the morning print-out was brought to this rabid weasel.

She studied the uniform he wore, the debonair loose trousers, the neat boots, the short-waisted green jacket. He was near her size. She noted that the black plastic pistol sat loose in its holster, as if the Reg had been playing gunslinger again.

She reached into her coat pocket and removed the precious flask of clean water. After taking a long drink, she positioned it for a strategic spill. With a brush of the hand, the water hit the crack in the decaying power cord. Sparks flew, the computer crackled, fizzed. Whit jumped away. The machine made a resounding pop and quickly became a box of flames, scorching the memory chips beyond reclamation.

The Reg was beside her, yelling. Whit pointed at the supply closet, shouted that the fire extinguisher was inside. The Reg opened the door and hurried inside, back turned.

So stupid, Whit thought, delivering the knock-out blow.

*****

Amelia felt through the soft earth until her fingers met a familiar lump. She dug out the potato and dropped it in the reed basket by her side. Far away, she heard the distant drone of an engine.

She paused, looked up in alarm, and searched the smoky, yellow layers of pollution that hung overhead. A rivulet of July sweat trickled down the side of her tanned face.

There was a sudden flash of light in the east, and a shape was hurtling toward her, lower and still lower in the sky. The glinting, metal craft seemed to be heading right for the potato field.

She sprang up, incensed. Chicago Regulators had already stolen her Spring barley. Now they were obviously returning for her potatoes.

The craft roared closer. As Amelia shaded her eyes to better see, she realized that this particular jetcraft was twisting and darting from side to side, clearly out of control. With a cry of fear, Amelia began racing for the irrigation ditch at the edge of the field.

She dove into the muddy trench as the jetcraft belly-whopped across the earth. The ground shook, dust clouds rolled, jet fuel sprayed into the air. And then the summer stillness fell again. Amelia peered over the edge of grassy weeds, waiting in dread.

These days the jetcrafts were patched-together conglomerations of any usable piece of machinery a mechanic could find. They featured steel, aluminum, graphite, even burned metal areas, for most of the parts were foraged from crash sites. Proving to be no exception, this downed model showed its century of use.

Just as she was ready to climb out of the ditch, the jet door clanked open and a Regulator fell into the dirt. The man stood up and made a high-pitched, cursing sound as the first steps were taken. Amelia slid down into the rank water at the bottom of the ditch, her stomach cramping with fear.

If this man found her he would kill her. He was not here to steal fresh vegetables. He had just crash-landed, destroying an irreplaceable machine. The Reg's misfortune would undoubtedly result in some harsh punishment by his Tribune, a punishment of ghastly torture. And Regs were known for venting their frustrations on the first woman they saw.

The cursing Reg came nearer. Amelia found herself listening to the odd voice, wondering at words she didn't recognize. Then, all at once, there was a deafening blast and a body plowed into her, dunking her in the ditch water.

Amelia lurched out of the shallow water, sputtering, her ears ringing. The body against her rolled clear, right into the mud bank.

The Reg cap had been lost in the fall and long, dark hair fell wet across straight, broad shoulders. Gray eyes stared back at her.

Moments slid by. Both were speechless.

The Reg finally glanced up at the sky with a nervous expression. Suddenly, Amelia was no longer afraid.

This was no Regulator, despite the uniform. This was a woman! But women were serfs, they were either Farmers or Breeders, depending on whether or not they had been exposed to the disease. So why was this woman wearing a Regulator's uniform? Was this an escape? Amelia's mind braked in confusion.

There was no escape from Elysium. The Border made sure of that.

Whit rose painfully, ignoring the Farmer, and limped to the far side of the ditch. She tried to scale the bank but froze halfway up, hissing with pain. Amelia stood, and before she knew what she was doing, pushed the slim hips over the crest, into the grass. Eyes wary, the injured woman looked down at her.

What a face this woman had! High aristocratic cheekbones, sculpted hollows below them, a fine, thin nose. Inner strength showed in the set of her full lips, the fierce look in her grey eyes. She did not look feminine, not at all.

The word echoed through Amelia's mind again. *Escape.* On an impulse, she scrambled out of the ditch, helped the woman up and declared, "I have hiding places."

Whit shook her head, protesting, "They'll kill you."

Amelia searched the sky. "I'm dead anyway. You landed in my field." In an official monotone she stated, "'There are no accidents.'"

Whit almost smiled at that, then caught herself and gave Amelia a measuring stare. "I can't take you with me."

Take me where? Amelia thought. *Take me to my death? I just told her the crash alone had already condemned me. The fact that she came here makes me part of her crimes.*

Amelia swept her eyes across the scene before them. The heli-jet's fiery remains were strewn across Baubo's farm and its fragrant brown soil. The jet fuel had no doubt ruined part of the land. So much for the potato crop. So much for everything she had ever known.

Amelia sighed. Then she took Whit's arm, draped it around her shoulders and began the walk through the apple orchard.

"I mean it," Whit said, with a grimace of pain. "I can't take you."

"I think it is me who is taking you."

"I can walk," the strange woman insisted, trying to free herself from Amelia's grasp.

"Your knee is injured."

As Whit shook her head no, she caught her foot on a vine and gasped. After that, Amelia gradually felt more of the taller woman's weight shift onto her shoulders. Whit stayed silent, studying the grove of trees ahead.

In the distance, they both heard a heli-jet approaching.

Whit thought quickly and said, "There should be a cluster of rocks nearby."

"Behind the house," Amelia replied, and thought, *How does **she** know about the group of granite boulders near the Border?*

"Take me there," Whit commanded.

"The house will be the first place they'll look," Amelia said simply.

"Are you going to argue over everything? Take me there!" Whit insisted.

"No!"

Whit stopped and faced her angrily. "Then we part company, Castewoman."

Amelia let go of Whit's hand, shrugged off her arm. Whit limped a few steps, then turned and demanded, "Which way?"

As the heli-jet passed overhead, they both instinctively ducked beneath a tree and hid. The engine sounded labored from years of wear, and though the copter hovered crazily over the potato field, as if about to crash, it successfully landed. They heard the engine chug and then die.

The woman looked at her desperately. Amelia pointed the direction, then watched the stranger's ragged, uneven gait. In spite of herself, her anger dissolved. She caught up and ducked under a flailing arm.

"I don't need help! At least go try to hide!" Whit snapped.

Amelia glared at her.

Whit shook her head, muttering words Amelia had never heard before, words spoken like curses.

Amelia steered them through the scrub forest, winding through saplings. She thought she smelled the harsh, unwashed scent of a man. Maybe it was only the stolen uniform this strange woman wore. All the same, the hair at the back of her neck stood on end.

Whit pulled Amelia to a stop, scrutinizing the small, square structure. "You live in that?" The voice was flat, disgusted.

Amelia fumed. This stranger obviously had no idea what it had taken for her and Baubo to build their house. They had spent months digging in the old, abandoned landfills around Chicago. They had risked death by lurking around a government construction site. Baubo had made her stay silent in the wagon while she sweet-talked the laborers, bartering corn whiskey for concrete. Amelia could still remember the laborers eyeing her longingly, then scuttling away when they saw the AGH tatoo on her wrist.

The house was a mish-mash of another century, suspended in concrete. Once, there had been enough oil to make plastic, enough plastic to be thrown away. The countless old containers, empty now of detergent or juice, provided the insulation of ready-made air pockets and sealed winter from them when it came. Strips of torn and dented vinyl siding had been hammered into a slanting roof. It looked grotesque, but the house was warm and dry.

"Where is Baubo?" Whit asked hurriedly, looking around.

"Those are her burial stones." Amelia nodded her head at the circle of rocks surrounding a mound of green grass.

Whit covered her heart with her hand. To Amelia it looked like some sort of salute. *How does this stranger know Baubo?*

Twigs cracked in the brush nearby. The man-smell came again, rank, close. Amelia glanced back apprehensively. Suddenly, a fine, rope net soared through the air, then fell over them. They were wrenched off their feet before they could do more than cry out. In another second the huge Regulator was towering over them, laughing lasciviously.

"One diseased and feeble-minded peasant, and one Freeland warrior, virgin clean."

Freeland warrior? Amelia thought confusedly. This coiled knot of tense womanhood next to her was a Freeland warrior? *Could Baubo's tales be true?*

"You've been rolling in mud and you both look like pigs." The Reg kicked Amelia, growling, "Are you the dummy? I don't want the slow death because my organ got into dirty pussy."

He reached beneath the mesh and seized Amelia's arm. She clutched the net, frantically, uselessly resisting.

And then the warrior woman said, quite wearily, "We have no AGH in Freeland, idiot."

Freeland! Amelia thought. *It was no myth!*

The Regulator dropped the Castewoman and grabbed the warrior, obviously overwrought with lust. The net fell. Amelia immediately began scrambling to get out of the tangle, but the other Reg grabbed her from behind, laughing, and pulled her against his body and hard organ.

Whit wrestled with her own would-be rapist, trying to pull the gun from her holster. Smacking her hand aside, the Regulator grabbed her gun and flung it away. Not giving up, she reached for her short sword, but the Regulator wrenched it away from her, laughing as if this were great sport.

Ignoring the pain in her wounded leg, the warrior woman landed a series of hard snap-kicks to the shins and knees of the barrel-chested Reg. He stopped laughing. He snarled, swinging his sword angrily. Whit danced aside expertly. The Reg lost his balance and the sword went all the way to the ground, its razor-sharp blade parting the nylon net inches from Amelia's body and the Reg holding her.

Whit continued her attack with spirited yells, kicking the guard in the head repeatedly, until a loud and final "Ooof" came from him. The beefy Regulator collapsed, and Whit sank to the ground in pain.

Twisting free from the grasp of the Regulator who was holding her, Amelia slithered through the opening the sword had made in the net. She scrambled to her feet and stomped her captor's ankle with all the power she could muster. Next, she lunged for the pistol that had been knocked from the warrior woman's hand. But before she could grab the gun, the Reg was upon her. He spun her around so she was facing him, and for a moment Amelia stood frozen, held by his menacing gaze

As the Reg raised his sword to deal a death blow to Amelia, the warrior woman moved swiftly behind him. Like a jackhammer, she kicked him in the back, in the right kidney, then in the left kidney, launching the man forward. Amelia's fist met his nose before she realized she had moved.

They went round and round for several minutes like that, the two women landing blows from either side of him, darting clear of his sword. He was far more powerful, but they were faster—hitting vital areas and leaping aside before he could counter.

Amelia found her body streaking through motions with a will of its own, unleashing graceful strokes of violence she had not known she could produce. More than once, the Freeland warrior glanced at her, eyes wide with amazement, as Amelia began to mimic the warrior's own fighting style.

Then the Regulator bellowed and threw his sword at Amelia's head. She reeled away, but the fire across the top of her right arm told her he had made enough of a hit. She went dizzy, and felt herself crumpling to the ground.

The grass was soft and damp against her cheek. She opened her eyes and saw the Regulator grab the warrior's foot as she snap-kicked. He dropped her, roaring with triumph, as she attempted to twist her leg free from his strong grasp. He struck the warrior woman senseless, then quickly unzipped the front of his pants, sniggering with glee.

Amelia saw the sunlight slanting through tree branches above them, saw the sword lying a few feet away, gleaming. Her own blood colored the metal edge, calling her.

Somehow, she was standing behind the man. She raised her good arm, clenching the discarded weapon like a dagger.

The Freeland warrior opened her eyes and focused on the man ripping off her clothes, then on the plunging sword.

— 2 —

The Reg fell sideways.

Whit scooted away from him, eyes riveted on his astonished face. She gazed numbly at his sagging erection, at her borrowed trousers bunched about her knees.

She looked up at the Farmer swaying on her feet a short distance away. Amelia's white face was a stark contrast to the streaks of ditch mud across it. An awful stream of blood was flowing from her shoulder.

Whit got to her feet, securing her trousers, glancing at the rock fall. She thought, *It's the law. I have to leave her. Just find the plate and go.*

Instead, she went to the Farmer and hooked the woman's good arm around her own powerful shoulders, just as the woman had done with her. Painfully, Whit dragged them both across the grass, feeling resolute and stubborn.

In between the boulders, concealed by thick weeds, Whit found the smooth crystalline surface she sought. Just as Whit's hand touched it, automatically unlocking the gate with her DNA code, the Farmer raised her head. "I want to go home," she mumbled, and then went limp. Whit stepped through the Bordergate with the Farmer, thankful the Elysian was light.

For several minutes she felt nothing but the humming vibration of the screen, then she emerged into the Wilderness on the other side. She was bruised and exhausted and delighted to see blue, not yellow, sky overhead.

Settling the Castewoman in tall grass, she checked her wound. Ditch mud and blood were already clotting together, but the cut looked deep. Whit scouted the landscape and spotted the solar panels marking the first crosser's cache.

Sliding the door open, she entered the dome structure. She switched on the small computer, intent on sending a message to Cimbri in Artemis, by bouncing another beam to the telecommunications satellite. Then, after a long moment of waiting, Whit disappointedly discovered that the storage battery was dead. When she went outside to determine why, she couldn't believe her eyes. The feeder wires from the solar panels had been sliced into many pieces. The small satellite dish on the roof had been mangled beyond repair.

She cursed loudly for several minutes. It was such a joy to indulge in a bad temper again. Thank the Goddess she could leave obedient, fearful, female behavior behind her now.

Whit shook off the tantrum, went back into the dome and made a quick inventory of the supplies housed in the Border Station. Plenty of food and travel items. She grabbed up the medical kit and a water pail, trying to recall the field training she had received.

Finding the Farmer still unconscious, the warrior woman decided the first order of business was cleaning the sword wound. She left the woman long enough to find the gurgling stream, fill the pail and deposit it on a hastily made fire to boil. She carried the med-kit to the water's edge, then she went and gathered the Castewoman up like a lanky dog on its way to a bath.

Whit laid the woman on the soft, grassy stream bank, tore away the tattered peasant dress and the much-mended slip beneath it. While she waited for the water to heat, she checked the contents of the med-kit and wished she had something to eat. Whit found herself studying the Elysian's lean, muscled thighs, the thatch of blonde hair above, then noted the AGH tatoo on the wrist. Whit grimaced. *What a pity.* Now the raised, purplish lesions on the Farmer's arms and legs seemed very apparent. *It's been a long time since I've let myself look at a woman,* Whit realized.

Retrieving the pail of hot water, she positioned it within reach, then knelt down beside the peasant woman. Deftly, she squirted astringent soap into the med-kit sponge. At the first gentle scrub the Farmer's lolling head shot up, her voice a wail of shock, her brown eyes glazed. Whit went after the wound with the astringent, digging into the red slice of tissue without mercy. The Castewoman grabbed at Whit's hands, trying to stop her, then finally leaned against Whit, helpless, while she quickly cleansed every inch of the thin, wiry body. Whit hesitated, then took time to rinse Amelia's muddy hair in the last of the heated water.

A fresh cloth was plucked from the med kit, and then dipped in the icy stream. She pressed the cold cloth against the Castewoman's wound, hoping to staunch the steady flow of blood.

Mother, what if she goes into shock?

Whit snatched up the med-kit and hustled back to the dome. She rooted around until she found the sleeping bags she knew would be there. Opening all four of them, she spread them out on the hard, plastic floor, then limped back to the stream bank.

She knelt and took the peasant woman in her arms. With a grunt, she lifted her, gritting her teeth against the pain in her knee.

The Farmer roused a little, pointed weakly at the bank, at the trees there. "Willow bark. Boil it..." she whispered.

Whit looked into the half-lidded, cow eyes and an odd fluttering sensation streaked through the center of her.

"Boil it," the woman insisted weakly.

Then the eyes closed and Whit felt as if she had been released from an electrical current. She surveyed the trees and then in a huff of superiority, turned away from them. Carrying the Farmer, she staggered back to the cache dome.

Inside, Whit worked quickly, dabbing salve into the trickling gash, pressing the bandage down and wrapping the shoulder tightly.

Her hands moved over the still form, acutely aware of the defined, hardened muscles. She wrapped the woman in a protective cocoon of sleeping bags and made herself ignore the ocean wave of arousal rising within her.

Then she was able to pay attention to her own needs. The smelly uniform joined the peasant clothes at the water's edge. Wading into the stream, Whit immersed herself for a chilling but much needed wash.

Back at the cache dome, she found warrior clothing and happily donned the familiar soft, beige outfit. She built a fire at the door of the shelter and made herself some long-missed oatmeal. She considered going out after the bark the Castewoman had wanted, then, feeling warm and sleepy and content, she remembered what the Reg had said.

The Reg had called the peasant "dummy." Whatever else might be wrong in Elysium, the Reg files were insidiously accurate. Their mechanical equipment was laughably out of date and in poor repair; the education system was pathetic and health care nonexistent, but the data from Reg Dispatch was almost infallibly correct.

The trees by the water were just trees. Whit lay down in the firelight and watched the Castewoman sleep.

Her hair was drying, now, turning the color of ripe corn. The smooth face was pleasing—sunburned cheeks and a straight, elegant nose. The lips were parted. She looked young and defenseless.

Yet, this Farmer had fought beside her like a trained Freeland warrior. This Farmer had fallen, severely wounded, and had still managed to slay a Reg.

In two years, no Elysian had ever done so much as a small favor for Whit. No one had ever given her a spoonful of beans when she was hungry, a drink of water when she was thirsty. Elysians lived in self-isolation, in fear. All, except it seemed, this Farmer, who had unaccountably saved her life. This was certainly the most peculiar Elysian she had ever met.

Whit frowned. Against all rules, she had brought this Castewoman through the Bordergate. And that angelic face had not looked so angelic during the fight with the Reg.

Oh, Mother, what have I done, now? Whit wondered. *There will be hell to pay for this!*

*****

In the morning the Castewoman was delirious. She repeatedly threw off the covers and tried to get up, mumbling that she had to go home. Whit began to worry about her feeble medical knowledge. It finally occurred to her that the willow bark was worth a try. Whit boiled a tea and held the Farmer tight, forcing her to swallow it.

By evening the Farmer knew Whit again. She noticed the wood shavings in the cup and sleepily told Whit the tea would heal the swelling in her knee. Whit glanced down at her loose britches, wondering how the woman knew her knee was badly swollen. While the peasant woman slept, Whit reluctantly took a dose of the awful-tasting medicine.

*****

The warrior leaned over Amelia, gently tugging the dressing free of the dried blood beneath it. Amelia hunched, gripping the blankets, leaning her forehead into bent knees.

"I killed him, didn't I?" Amelia rasped.

"The Reg? Yes."

A tremor overcame her as she recalled the feel of the sword sinking into flesh and sinew.

"He would have eventually killed both of us. The Regs are walking dung," the warrior pronounced.

Amelia sighed. This strange woman sounded like an arrogant Reg herself—people died because they deserved it. She muttered, "You've...killed?"

"As hideous as violence is, there are savages loose in the world. A woman who does not fight back will not be free."

Amelia asked again, "Have you killed?"

A pause, then, "No."

Amelia let her silence tell the woman that opinions without experience were pretty much worthless. Whit paid no attention. The nuances of unspoken dialogue seemed beyond her.

Amelia looked around at their odd shelter. They seemed to be in an upside-down bowl. "Where are we?"

The warrior stopped for an instant, then peeled the last of the bandage away. Amelia felt as if a layer of her flesh went with it. She didn't scream, but the effort not to, exhausted her. A warm gush of blood was trickling down her back.

Feeling bewildered and sluggish, she added, "We can't be on Baubo's land. The Regulators would have dropped the nerve gas long ago. What happened? Where *are* we?"

A soft, moist cloth mopped at the mess on her back. A cooling, anti-bacterial powder met the heat of the slash mark, and though the fingers barely touched her, Amelia felt as if she had been lanced. She made no sound, but the way she jerked away betrayed her.

The warrior said, "Easy. We're in Freeland. We crossed."

"Crossed?"

The warrior said, "There's a Bordergate at the edge of Baubo's farm."

More powder came against the steadily leaking cut. Amelia began to feel as if she were floating.

"Who are you?" Amelia asked, with a fading voice.

"Major Tomyris Whitaker. Please call me Whit. And who are you?" The tone was light, almost mocking.

"Amelia," she whispered.

"Just Amelia?" the warrior asked.

Nodding her head was difficult. Saying the words was even harder. "You knew Baubo. How? How did we penetrate the Border?"

"So many questions," the warrior chuckled, as she fitted a fresh bandage against her skin. "I have to stop this bleeding. I'm sorry." Without further warning, the warrior pressed down hard. A cry launched out of Amelia. The haze that had been forming around the edges of her mind came rolling in like a river fog. She felt the warrior wrapping her arm, felt herself being lowered, and then tucked beneath blankets again. And despite the fog, she was sure she felt a gentle hand slip slowly through her hair.

*****

Amelia shoved her arm into the butter-soft fabric, anxious to get herself covered as quickly as possible.

On the other side of her, Whit carefully guided the injured arm through a sleeve, warning, "If you start this shoulder bleeding again, I'll make you drink more of that swill you call tea."

Amelia bent her head, feeling the heat in her face, knowing she was a human strawberry. She pulled the shirt closed, frantic to hide her chest.

Whit knelt before her and flapped the two sides out of her grasp, pronouncing, "Too big. Mother, you're a flat-chested woman."

Outraged, Amelia snatched the shirt closed.

Whit tilted her head sideways, reaching for the buttons and saying, "No offense meant, Amelia."

The way Whit spoke her name made Amelia look at her again. Whit's face was close. The gray eyes were bright, focused on the buttons she was fastening. Her prominent cheekbones betrayed a warm flush of color. Amelia's anger stole away and left her puzzled.

"Let's try this," Whit said, moving the tan jacket toward her bad side.

Amelia clenched her teeth against the pain of lifting her arm and beads of sweat sprang out across her forehead. When the jacket was completely on, she was breathing hard and Whit was watching her intently.

"So when do we start the journey to Freeland?" Amelia asked, trying to mask just how much of an ordeal dressing had been for her.

The warrior's eyes changed, seemed to harden. "Don't rush it, Peasant. We've only been here a week. This journey won't be like bringing in the hay. Are you sure you're ready?"

Amelia stood, bristling at the patronizing tone. She reached for her knapsack and Whit lifted it away, smiling. The warrior strode ahead of her, gamely carrying the two knapsacks, leading the way into Freeland.

*****

Whit coolly observed Amelia's wonder at the world beyond the Border. She sniffed the air, bent over various plants and shrubs with astonished eyes, remarked with disbelief that the sky was blue. Whit told her that many things were possible when a century's worth of noxious fumes were not trying to filter through a dense molecular screen.

Days passed, nights passed. They followed a deer trail through a forest of thick-trunked trees, then marched through a broad valley of grass. High weeds snagged around their boots and Whit went from a proud, whistling figure to a limping, silent grump. Amelia's fever came and went, slowing her efforts, frustrating her determination to prove her worth.

At last, Whit gave in to her knee and announced they would camp for a full day's rest. Amelia used the willow bark she had packed to brew them a huge pot of Whit's most unfavorite beverage, then hounded Whit into drinking cup after cup. By nightfall, they were both restless.

Whit pulled out a map she had stolen before her mad dash from Elysium. It was old and brittle, but at least it would provide them with a trail to follow. Whit began studying the old railway markings. The grades and tunnels would make the trek so much easier.

Amelia pointed at the red lines marking highways and asked why they didn't find a car and follow one of the roads. Whit told her in a clipped, haughty voice that the only cars they would find were the disintegrating remnants of Pre-Schism times. And with no gasoline, what good would a car be to them?

Whit took a small stick from the fire and blew on it to cool the burned end. "We're in what was once known as Nebraska," she grumbled, then poked the stick at the right spot on the map when Amelia didn't seem to know where to look. "We're about two thousand miles from the closest colonies. No one lives out here."

"Why not? Don't you have Farmers?"

"Our Farmers are allowed to be citizens. They live near their colony." Whit made a long-suffering sigh and swept her hand across the states east of the Nebraska. "See? This is Elysium." She moved the hand to the states along the west coast. "And this is Freeland. We used to be all one nation, before the AGH plague. Now it's Elysium in the East, the Wilderness in the middle and the seven city-colonies of Freeland in the West."

"City-colonies?"

The gray eyes studied Amelia with impatience. She rattled off odd-sounding names, marking four spots on the west coast, three spots in the southwest.

"But there's so much empty land," Amelia protested. "Why?"

"Because so many died!" Whit barked. "Because you Elysians chased out everyone who wasn't white and heterosexual and healthy! The plague was ten times worse out here, and all you Elysians could think of was constructing your stupid biosphere screen!"

Amelia nearly shouted back at her, caught herself, and pressed her lips together instead. In Elysium, there were women without tongues. She would have to see if everyone in Freeland were allowed such childish outbursts, before she dared to mimic the rude warrior.

Whit went back to plotting a course and Amelia sat silent, watching. After a while, seeing Whit's northern route developing, Amelia asked why they didn't go south, in case the autumn came with early snows. Whit took her charcoaled stick and made a huge x across what had once been Colorado, Utah and Nevada.

"It's toxic," Whit sighed, as if Amelia were incredibly ignorant.

Amelia stared at the huge section of map. "Toxic?"

"Hydrogen bomb. Just one," Whit answered.

Amelia sat back, horrified. "Regs?"

"No, their bosses, the New Order Christians. It happened during the Great Schism. They said they were cleansing the earth. Some cleansing."

Amelia remembered the preacher who had appeared on the farm one day, clomping heedlessly across the small herb garden she was weeding. He had heard that Baubo was a healer, and that meant that she could also be a witch. Amelia remembered kneeling there, afraid, unable to manage the prayer-words he kept repeating at her. He had shown her a smooth, woodcarved cross on a leather thong and then placed it around her neck. He had spoken kindly to her, running his hands down her arms, until he saw the tatoo. Then he had cursed and hit her, until she cried out. Baubo had finally come, had given the man assurances and a sack full of carrots. The preacher, after looking at the women contemptuously, abruptly left. And then Baubo had taken the cross from Amelia's neck and flung it in the dirt.

Whit broke into her thoughts. "Your name," she said. "It's a Christian name."

Amelia frowned, but did not respond.

Whit concentrated on the map again.

The question popped out before Amelia could stop it. "Why were you in Elysium?"

No answer.

"Why was the Reg chasing you? What did you do?"

Whit sullenly stared at the map.

After several minutes of abrasive silence, Whit stood and tossed more wood on the fire. "I have already broken the law and risked my rank by bringing a diseased Castewoman across the border. I draw the line at divulging Freeland secrets to a curious peasant girl," Whit spat out.

Amelia sniffed and replied, with an air of confidence, "A peasant's tea has healed your leg." Disarmed, Whit tested the leg. Then she asked about the tea. Amelia told her it was a secret.

Whit narrowed her eyes. "Clearly, you are not 'feebleminded.' How did you fool the Regs?"

"Some believe the worst about people," Amelia answered smugly. She calmly unfurled her sleeping bag near the fire and set about going to sleep.

Whit stared at her stubborn back and worried.

*****

They followed the slight mound of earth and rusting steel track that had once been a major railroad line into the Pacific Northwest. After two weeks, they left flat Nebraska behind and entered mountainous Wyoming. The late July skies were cobalt blue and cloudless. Aspen leaves flickered in the slightest of breezes, making each stir of wind a shimmering event. The air smelled sweet with summer and the birds twittered and called from daybreak to dusk.

They rarely talked because they were both struggling. Trying to distract herself from the ache she felt with each stride, Whit sang ribald marching songs about voluptuous women. After a few days, Amelia was singing along with the choruses, though Whit doubted that she understood what cunnilingus meant.

Each night Whit changed Amelia's bandages and each night her eyes lingered longer on the planes of her smooth back. The skin lesions Whit had noticed weeks ago, seemed to be fading, but she firmly reminded herself that this Elysian carried disease. She knew how AGH was gotten and how it mercilessly destroyed its victims.

In Freeland, they had developed a cure, a vaccine that boosted the immune system's resistance. But the sterile safety of Cimbri's clinic was very far away from her now, and Whit had begun to doubt her own immunity.

By now, the anxiety in the woman's manner whenever Whit touched her was unmistakable. Amelia's modesty bordered on shame. From what she knew of Elysium, Whit decided that Amelia's AGH had probably been the product of a rape. Whit resolved to keep her reawakening desires under control until she was back in Artemis. The unashamedly sexual women along the Sound would welcome her home, soon enough.

But it still surprised her, how much she was beginning to like this Elysian. She wondered how long Amelia had lived with Baubo, if she was "the apprentice" Baubo referred to in her cryptic messages to Lilith.

"I have found the apprentice", the first transmission had said, ten years ago. "The apprentice is nearly ready", the last transmission had stated. *When was that? Last December?*

Whit had never been briefed on just what Baubo was doing in Elysium. She only knew that the old woman had disappeared beyond the Border ten years ago, that the farm she worked as a lowly peasant was the section of Elysian land that contained the northern Bordergate.

The more southerly Bordergate was the entrance and exit of choice. The comings and goings of Freeland warriors were easy to conceal in the deep Louisiana bayous. No one used the northern gate, no one wanted to risk appearing out of nowhere on the Nebraska plains, so clearly visible to the watchful informants of the Chicago Regs. Whit had only used the gate because the stolen heli-jet had malfunctioned early and going north was the shorter route.

Whatever Baubo's mission, it had been important enough to keep her in Elysium for ten years, until she had died there, far from home and her countrywomen. Whit could not imagine enduring such a long exile.

And what had this unknown apprentice been learning from Baubo? Psychic dabblings and healing had been Baubo's preoccupation in Artemis, where she had taught intuitive sensitivity and cast Runes for the lovelorn. Of what worth was that? It was called witchcraft in Elysium.

Without understanding why, Whit gradually became certain that Amelia was the apprentice. But Amelia seemed as practical and rooted to the earth as Whit herself. This was no air-headed spiritualist. It made no sense.

Eventually, Whit realized she was dying to ask Amelia if the old woman had taught her more than the evident knowledge of plants. Had she taught her about the desires of certain women, too?

After all, there were no lesbians in Elysium. The women were all Farmers or Breeders there. Anyone displaying a hint of sexually outlawed behavior was arrested. The official line held that lesbians were not only a waste of a womb, but a possible corruption of their fellow females. So they were systematically tortured and killed. Like some insect pest, they were systematically hunted down and stamped out on sight.

By the fourth week of their arduous trek, Whit had noticed quite a lot about Amelia.

The woman just didn't carry herself like an Elysian. The rigid circumspection was there, but it was an act and it fell from her at the oddest times—when she was playing with Whit's compass, fascinated, voluble with questions—when she was gathering weeds, exclaiming about the abundant species; while she was watching the sunset, deeply entranced with the colorful day's end.

Elysians didn't care about scientific toys or plants or sunsets. They were cold, beaten-down, mean-natured. Had Baubo taught this girl what it was to be human?

Someone had. The woman was a volcano of emotion beneath that placid exterior. It made Whit feel strangely excited, strangely afraid.

And then there were her teeth.

Elysians had bad teeth. It was the most highly visible sign of their loss of civilization. In Elysium, the formula for something as simple as an enamel sealant was unknown. Whit's teeth were straight, strong, and white and she had just spent two years continually keeping her mouth shut in order to avoid notice.

Amelia, by all rights, should have been noticeably missing some teeth. Yet, not only did she have them all—they were perfect, white, undamaged. Like Whit's own.

Whit could think of no explanation for it.

The questions Whit wouldn't answer now caused Amelia to turn aside Whit's own questions, and Whit was too proud to redress the situation. Her curiosity became a churning, silent entity, shadowing her throughout the day.

As they journeyed, the bitter malice towards Elysians that had once consumed Whit began to pass. The flashes of helpless anger at the Castewoman, using her as a target for her feelings about the entire Elysian culture, came less and less often. The clean air and fresh, pollution-free landscape gradually washed Whit clean. She fell into a quiet, affable acceptance of the mysterious Farmer woman.

During the chilly nights when the fire burnt low, Amelia began huddling against her, seeking the warmth of Whit's firm body in the grogginess of sleep. Whit often found herself gently stroking Amelia's cornsilk hair, hair that gleamed even in the thin light of the stars. She longed to kiss this Farmer woman, longed to feel her respond with that strength that showed so often in the set of her jaw. Instead, Whit snuggled closer and made herself accept her role as bed-warmer.

It had to be enough. The woman carried AGH.

— 3 —

Three long weeks later, Whit stood at the top of a ridge, breathing hard. The jagged crests of the Rocky Mountains rimmed the horizon like teeth in the maw of a shark. A more insurmountable barrier Whit could not imagine.

All along the narrow rise where she waited, the Ponderosa pines began to bend in the stiff wind. She looked to the northwest and saw dark clouds boiling, rolling over each other, racing across the valley toward her. She had to find the next crosser's cache quickly.

Amelia—head down, engrossed in the effort to climb the steep hillside—stumbled into her. For an instant, Whit's boots skidded helplessly on loose gravel and earth, then Amelia seized her arm. Whit ended up lying on the sixty degree incline, gasping, staring at the sharp drop beyond her boots.

Above her, Amelia was stretched on her belly, hugging a small boulder with one arm, grasping Whit with the other. A low groan emanated from her.

Trying not to draw on Amelia's hold, Whit carefully crawled back up. She squirmed to Amelia's side and lay beside her. "Sweet Mother!" Whit panted. "Where is your mind?!"

A roll of thunder echoed across the valley.

Whit sat up and scanned the ridge. "We've got to get off this high ground before the storm hits. The crosser's cave is supposed to be directly below here. If we can find it, we'll have shelter and a new ration of food."

Out of habit, Whit lifted the edge of Amelia's knapsack, looking for telltale signs of new bleeding. Pushing her hand away, Amelia quickly got to her feet. She was hurt by Whit's sarcasm, not quite understanding why Whit's opinion of her mattered so much.

They hiked about a quarter mile along the ridge, until they found an outcropping of rock that allowed a more gradual descent. As they hurried down, Whit spotted the cave with relief. Then a sound floated above them, a sound almost like one a woman would make.

Amelia whirled.

"Cat," Whit stated, casting her eyes searchingly over the numerous ledges between them and the cave.

Thunder came, a dull roar of it, much nearer this time.

"There aren't any cats, any more," Amelia said.

"Not in Elysium, but here, we have plenty." Whit gathered several fist-sized rocks and walked ahead, shouting loudly.

"Don't," Amelia complained. "I want to see it."

"It may be the last thing you see," Whit said, nervously.

Amelia frowned, clearly not following the implication. Whit told her, "This cat is looking for a meal."

"Cats eat mice. Baubo told me."

Whit laughed. "In the colonies there are mice-eating cats, but in the mountains—"

Above them, a large, tawny cougar glided gracefully from one ledge to another. Amelia's jaw dropped. Whit tossed a rock, hollered "Run," and darted for the cave.

They hustled through the entrance, tumbled over each other, slammed into the stony floor. Whit leapt up and dove for the computer. The storm outside overtook the sun and the light in the cave faded into a murkiness.

Whit immediately keyed the computer into the operations-mode. She then set up an electronic force field before the door that would protect them from the cat as well as the storm. Finally, she set environment functions to warmth and light. Within seconds, the lamps overhead were glowing cheerfully. The cat sniffed at the shield, then padded away.

Whit heaved a sigh of relief, then turned and laughed at Amelia. "You're the clumsiest woman!"

Amelia lay on her back, the knapsack cockeyed beneath her. A crimson blotch on her beige warrior's shirt seemed to double in size as Whit spoke.

Whit dropped beside her. "Oh, no...oh, no." The raw edge of panic overtook Whit as she eased the pack from her. "Just when it seemed to be healing. You did this when you caught me on the ridge."

Amelia nodded and started mumbling an apology. Whit shushed her, pulling her up, trying to peel the shirt off before Amelia lost what was left of her strength.

By the time Whit had located the new medical kit and gotten the blood-soaked bandage off, Amelia was sinking against her, spent. Whit did what she could, then used the cache computer to send an S.O.S. to Artemis.

Amazed and frightened when no one answered her distress call, Whit passed the night listening to crashing thunder and gently stroking Amelia's corn-silk hair.

*****

Visibly pale, Amelia gazed into the fire Whit had built. It had been two days, now, since the cache computer battery had failed, its power inexplicably low for a seldom-used emergency station. A week ago they had arrived at the cave, out-running a rainstorm and a cougar. The thunderstorms had visited every day since then, and so had the cat.

Earlier, Amelia had speculated that they must be using his den. Whit had stated, face averted, that he had smelled the blood.

Her blood. Amelia had been more comfortable thinking that this was a housing dispute.

Whit seemed to be deeply troubled, but would only tell her that the computer had never been fully functional. Apparently, Whit had relied on the machine to perform some specific task, counting upon it to play some part in this long, rugged journey. Amelia was used to machines either failing or being used against her, so she was unfazed by their return to wood fires.

The loss of the force field, however, did bother her. She had not slept well since, anxious that the fire might burn too low and the cat might grow too brave.

Amelia gazed at the woman nestled against her, listened to the soft snore. Whit wasn't afraid of anything, sleeping easily until some small noise partially awakened her. Then those smoke-colored eyes blinked and she was awake—fully awake and ready. Amelia thought she had never seen anything like it, as she watched her.

The woman was a warrior, all right. She had known it was true as soon as the Regulator had said it. The tall, athletic build, the way she had moved—so effortlessly, gracefully strong. Even when limping, there had been a long-legged swagger to her gait.

Amelia studied the face and decided it was handsome. She had not initially thought her handsome, she had not even liked this woman, but she liked her now. She liked the teasing banter, the gruff affection, the genuinely thoughtful concern.

Whit had told her tonight that Artemis, her home colony, was a long way from here, deep in the Freeland Wilderness. Whit had said that without help, it was going to take months for them to reach it on foot.

Somehow, Amelia didn't mind. She was beginning to enjoy feeling Whit's hand in her hair when Whit thought she was asleep. She was beginning to feel certain she would miss being Whit's sole companion.

*****

Return to Isis

The next morning, the cougar ventured down into the valley and returned much later to nap in the shade of some pines. Noting the rounded belly, the bloodied muzzle and chest, Whit decided he had fed at last and that now they could risk resuming their journey without becoming dinner. She quickly packed up the new supplies and led them from the cave.

They kept a steady pace, feeling dwarfed by the mountains before them. The ridge rock turned to pebbles and then to desert sand. Each day the heat on the valley floor seemed more intense. At night they slipped their arms around each other, shivering beneath blankets, unable to find enough wood for a fire.

They no longer bickered, even when they were tired and thirsty. Working together, they learned to depend on each other's strengths. Whit fashioned a rope around Amelia's waist, lowering and hauling her over the edges of arroyos. Amelia milked the small cactuses they passed with a reedlike straw, gathering enough drinkable moisture for them to stay hydrated. They helped each other find the strength to keep moving, helped each other believe that they could endure this long and arduous journey.

When they reached the glacial streams of the mountain foothills, they rested another full day, dining on plants Amelia recognized. Then, on a warm, late August morning, they began climbing up into the fir forests.

*****

Nine weeks had passed since they had escaped from Elysium.

Whit knelt at the edge of the brook, dipping their canteens in the rushing water. She could hear Amelia thrashing about in the huckleberry bushes further up the slope. Whit resolved that later, no matter how tired she felt, she would look for any snakes Amelia hadn't scared completely off the mountainside. They were out of food packages, despite their careful rationing, and they were going to have to make use of any edible creature they encountered.

At the thought, she ran her eyes over the vegetation growing nearby, trying to recall what Amelia had told her to seek. Whit set the filled canteens aside, spotting some small cat tails that had managed to grow in a sunny section of marsh. She had her knife out and was digging for the tuberous roots when she heard the shouts of laughter, not far off.

*****

Someone behind her slung an arm around her throat and Amelia instinctively bent over. A body rolled over her back and into the berry bushes. Panicking, Amelia staggered away, clutching her reed basket. Several voices burst out laughing.

The figure she had thrown in the bushes came charging out, an inflamed face and grasping hands. Amelia dropped her basket and side-stepped, pushing the shoulders as the blur of motion passed. The shape sailed into the bushes on the other side of the small clearing. The laughter erupted again, wilder and louder.

The woman sprang out of the leafy branches, wiping scratches on her face and shouting a stream of harsh words. Amelia recognized some Freelandian curses she had heard from Whit. She noticed the clothing—many greens, not beige—but the outfit was otherwise identical to what Whit called a warrior's uniform. There was even a holstered gun on the woman's waist belt. Then, all at once, the woman dropped into a crouch, the way Whit had crouched when she had fought the Regulators.

Amelia held her arms straight out, as the Regulators had always required. "I beg pardon, I beg pardon."

"Elysium conduct!" the woman barked, looking shocked. "On your belly, Invader!"

"I—"

A kick in the stomach ended Amelia's explanation. She found herself face down in the grass, a foot grinding into her neck.

The woman hissed, "How did you cross the Border, Spy?"

Amelia yelped. Her unhealed shoulder was a raging fire.

Then, quite suddenly, the boot was gone and Whit was there, helping her roll over. The fierce woman sat nearby, rubbing her ear. Women began bursting from the bushes nearby.

Amelia watched their joy shower over Whit in hard embraces and thumps on the back. These were rough women, like men—no downcast eyes or submissiveness among them. And the skin colors, the hair! These were actually Africans and Indians, Mexicans, Japanese. The races of people that had survived Elysium's Aryan Decree of Racial Hygiene, just as Baubo had said.

They were dressed as she and Whit were dressed—brown boots that laced to the calf of the leg, high-collared shirts, short-waisted jackets and loose trousers—but each uniform was a design of multiple shades of green. No wonder she hadn't seen them in the bushes.

Amelia glanced at the arm of her beige jacket. *Camouflage?* She remembered the tan buffalo grass they had waded through in Nebraska.

"What happened?" an older looking woman demanded, grabbing Whit's hands. "The arrest posting came through on your transmission. We knew you were going to cross. Then we never heard from you. Lilith sent us to search, in case you were injured. When we traced no sign of you on the southern route we finally looked north..."

Whit swallowed hard, looking almost overcome by the reception. "I tried to signal, Branwen. Both cache computers malfunctioned."

A tall, copper-skinned woman interjected, "The cache computers on the southern route also showed signs of sabotage!"

"No trace of Elysians. It's really a mystery," another woman added.

Branwen rushed on, "We've been heat-seeking you for weeks, but the desert heat screwed up the instruments! We kept landing to explore false-possibles."

Amelia watched them intently. This woman Branwen was looking at Whit like...like the way the Regulators had often looked at Amelia herself, even after they saw the AGH tatoo on her wrist. It was that same intense, libidinous look.

Branwen glanced down at her, then back at Whit, then back down at Amelia. A questioning expression crossed her face.

Whit let go of Branwen's hands.

The woman who had attacked Amelia said, "The computers have never malfunctioned before."

Flicking a look at Amelia, Whit returned, "Let's discuss it later, Zoe."

Amelia surveyed this woman, Zoe. She was small compared to the others, slight of build. She had short, spiky brown hair and a turned-up nose. The only thing warrior-like about her was a pair of mean green eyes.

The copper-skinned woman spoke up again. "But all of the computers malfunctioning at the same time?"

"Elysians," Zoe hissed.

Whit shook her head no. "They still can't open the gates."

The mean green eyes landed on Amelia. "So then, why have you broken the law, Major, bringing this diseased peasant into our midst?"

Whit hesitated. Branwen, Zoe and the other twenty or so women warriors all waited expectantly. A grin stole across Whit's face and she shrugged. "I owe this peasant a field of potatoes."

They all laughed heartily at that. Amelia wondered if Whit would go back to making fun of her, now.

Then, Whit added seriously, "I also owe her my life. She took a sword thrust to the arm and still managed to drop the Reg about to rape me. I was quite effectively captured, quite disappointingly alive."

The other warriors made a murmuring noise of horror.

Whit finished softly, "If the Council faults me for bringing this woman through the Bordergate, I shall gladly endure the penance."

And with that, the tall, black-haired, woman with copper-colored skin reached down and helped Amelia to her feet. Amelia rose, hoping she wouldn't pass out in front of them all. The pain in her arm had become so excruciating that nothing else seemed real.

— 4 —

The transport ship had been left on a small plateau of meadow, several miles up the mountain. Zoe barked an order and the patrol of warriors began threading through the pines. Whit watched Nakotah take Amelia's pack from her, the black Sioux eyes honest with attraction. The contrast of blond hair and black hair, fair skin and canyon-red, walking side by side, was something Whit had not seen in two years. The sight shot exhilaration through her.

Oh, to be back in a land where beautiful women come in so many colors. Then she remembered Cimbri. Her heart fell.

Whit sent a glance at the woman moving gracefully beside her. Silver curled through the brown hair, creases had taken up residence in the fair skin around her eyes, but Branwen looked much the same. Still so aloof and serene.

Whit sighed. Her past was catching up with her, as Lilith had always said it would.

Branwen laughed. "Don't worry, Whit. I know that you have not come back for me."

Whit felt oddly disconcerted.

"I was only a means of restoring self-respect, wasn't I? Capturing the lone wolf." Branwen said.

"What?" Whit asked.

"You were running from Cimbri," Branwen whispered gently.

Stunned by her perception, Whit looked away.

Branwen went on, "It's alright. You were good for my image. Staid politician stalked by impetuous warrior, who then disappears into Elysium. Very romantic stuff, it turns out. Laid to rest my association with the infamous Maat. You'll be proud to hear I was elected Co-leader last year. I'm being seriously considered for election to the Freeland Senate. I have come far since you went off to play undercover agent in Elysium."

Whit sighed. She felt ashamed of the way she had treated Branwen, first pursuing, then discarding her.

Branwen murmured, "Besides, Cimbri is waiting for you."

Whit felt a lurch of anxiety. "Don't, Bran. Those days are autumn leaves."

Branwen calmly began relating what had been happening in Artemis. Whit didn't pay much attention until Branwen mentioned that Lilith showed the strain of leading the colony. Seeing Whit's interest, Branwen elaborated, "It seems that Lilith has been contending with Zoe."

Branwen whispered that Zoe had been striving to transform the Artemis unit of Freeland warriors into an offensive force. She was constantly referring to Isis, the mountain colony destroyed ten years ago by an invasion of Elysians. For months now, Zoe had been lobbying the Council, arguing that it was no longer enough to control the Border. Zoe was determined that an expeditionary force be sent into Elysium as a retaliation for that invasion. "You probably remember that Zoe's mother died at Isis, quite brutally. I think she's obsessed with shedding Elysian blood," Branwen ended.

Whit felt a stab of apprehension and looked for Amelia. Ahead, she saw Nakotah and Griffin flanking either side of the Castewoman, vying to entertain her. Amelia was quiet, looking up at each woman occasionally, but mostly walking along staring at the ground. The two warriors seemed very interested; Amelia seemed very tired. Whit felt like rushing up and pushing them away from her.

Jealousy, Whit thought, feeling mildly stricken by the realization. *And why not?* her reasoning called back. Amelia was striking, the kind of woman one's eyes kept returning to in a room full of prettier women. She was certainly not as unnervingly sensuous as Cimbri—yet Amelia's mind moved with a swallow's grace, integrity flashed in those deep brown eyes like sun-diamonds on a river. Amelia was going to be pursued in Artemis.

Whit brooded. Cimbri had taught her what love could be, what love could wreak within her. *I will not allow such utter madness to rule me again.*

Whit limped along, worn out and despondent.

A mountain meadow opened up before them and she saw the welcome sight of a steel patrol transport ship glittering in the sunlight. Whit had forgotten how sleek and shining aircraft were in Freeland. In the old assembly plants of Seattle, the women of Artemis had found enough information about planes to not only build their own, but to progress into a new era of methanol-fueled and electro-magnetic energy capabilities.

The party of Freeland warriors approached the vessel singing a jaunty hiking song. The only ones who did not sing were Amelia, who did not know the words, and Whit, who gazed sadly at Amelia's bright yellow hair from a small distance.

Returning to Artemis is turning out to be a mixed blessing, Whit thought ruefully.

*****

The transport ship crossed the Cascades and flew into Artemis just before sunset. Whit woke as they landed, and she nudged Amelia awake.

Amelia's sleepy brown eyes had barely opened when Zoe grabbed her, hauled her out of the flight chair, and dragged her across the cabin. Whit jumped up and went after them. With clipped words, Zoe ordered several of the warriors to hold Whit, who was by now furious at the way Amelia was being treated.

Zoe bellowed, "Elysians must be shackled in the city."

Whit laughed, although it came out more than a little wildly. "Zoe, that law is archaic. It's a pathetic remnant of the Great Schism!"

Zoe twisted Amelia's wounded arm behind her back, roughly pinning the Castewoman against the wall. "The Mothers left us the law," Zoe replied, vehemently. "And I, for one, do not break the law."

"No one even carries shackles, anymore!" Whit yelled.

With a flourish, Zoe produced a group of four cuffs and attaching lightweight chains. Amelia heard the jingling metal and seemed to go crazy—kicking and fighting Zoe.

Whit surged against the warriors who held her, shouting, "I out-rank Zoe! Stop this madness!"

"Sorry, Major," Nakotah returned, looking very sorry indeed. "The Captain has invoked the Security Measures. You have broken the law. This matter must be decided by the Council."

Amelia was landing terrified punches, easily overcoming the smaller woman. Her lip bleeding, Zoe retreated.

"Seize the Invader," she ordered harshly.

It took four women to wrestle Amelia down and keep her still long enough for Zoe to finally click the cuffs in place. All the while, Amelia yanked against the chains, whimpering, then fell back, exhausted, against the wall.

Zoe, her authority impugned, raised an arm and in a smooth arc backhanded Amelia across the face.

There was a uniform, sharp intake of breath. Many of the warriors took a step forward, uncertain about what to do, yet clearly disturbed, by Zoe's unwarranted brutality.

"You *Bitch!*" Whit screamed.

Zoe threatened in an icy voice, "You keep interfering and I'll..."

"You're abusing her!"

"Whitaker is under arrest," Zoe barked, as she pointed an accusatory finger at Whit.

"Captain, this is not—" Branwen began.

The small, red-faced woman swung around to face Branwen. "Co-Leader, I am in command of this patrol. I order her put in restraints." Zoe snatched up a second set of cuffs and tossed them to the unhappy Nakotah.

Whit made a growling noise and Nakotah whispered, "Don't resist, you'll just make her angrier. Lilith will settle this."

Whit maneuvered until she could see around the warriors. Amelia sat on the floor, expressionless, staring at the cuffs on her wrists. Branwen was leaning down, peering at her with puzzlement.

Zoe ordered everyone off the ship. She gripped her captive by the arm, cursing impatiently when Amelia couldn't keep up with her. Whit, too, tripped on the meager stretch of the ankle chains, but at least Nakotah had the decency to catch her before she fell. By the time the party of warriors had gotten across the landing zone, Whit had seen Amelia hit the stone pavement three times. Whit was so helpless with pent-up fury that she was crying.

"I demand Council, *now!*" Whit yelled at Zoe's back.

Zoe glanced over her shoulder, looking smug about the tears that quietly trickled down Whit's face. "In the morning. The Council does not meet on the demand of criminals. You will be held in containment overnight."

"*I DEMAND COUNCIL, NOW!!*" Whit roared.

Several mechanics near the ship hangars turned to stare, not quite believing what they were seeing. Nakotah shouted to them, "Call Lilith. Tell her Major Whitaker is back and demands Council."

"Tell her no such thing!" Zoe ordered. "You are on report, Lieutenant. I am in charge here!"

"Contact Lilith!" Branwen called. "Tell her Security Measures have been invoked by Captain Ference."

"You undermine my command, Co-leader!" Zoe hissed.

"Do you dare arrest me, too?" Branwen asked, smiling a lethal sort of smile. She crossed the tarmac to the hangar telecommunication panel and placed the call herself.

*****

Whit sat next to Amelia in the ceremonial Cedar House Council Chambers, watching for the arrival of the Council. Above them the thick cedar beams rose, cathedral-like, supporting the roof. Mahogany paneled walls were interspersed with walls of rosy, polished stone, more beautiful than marble. The floor was made of large, creamy white tiles. Colorful, richly embroidered district banners hung here and there, commemorating the champions of the Colony Games of past years. The Delphi emblem—a purple, six pointed star with a leaping dolphin in the center—hung on the wall behind the Leader's chair. To the right and left of the beautifully carved chair were doors leading to other chambers.

Whit looked around, feeling odd here in the center, surrounded by the huge, circular oak table. The continuous strip of light wood stretched all around her and Amelia, forming a complete, enclosing circle. But the circle did not make her feel safe. She had never been the one at the centerpoint, the one to have to sit in the chair, under charges, presenting a defense. It made Whit feel anxious and desperate to be here now after all she had endured to get back to Artemis. It was truly a Kafka-esque experience.

Hearing a soft groan come from Amelia, she looked with concern at the shackled young woman. The brown eyes were half-lidded, trance-like, aimed at the metal bands that held her arms. Whit asked again, "Are you alright?" And still no response. Amelia did not seem to hear her. The look of fever was unmistakable on her flushed, perspiring face.

A door swung open and the Council began to file into the room, moving to their individual places at the circular table. These were the fifty elected representatives, two from each district in Artemis, representing the combined population of roughly 1500 women. The Council members were a variety of ages, a variety of types: business executives in well-tailored suits, construction workers in dusty overalls, fisherwomen in thigh boots, shopkeepers wrapped in their store aprons, farmers sporting the eternal muddy trousers. Whit heard a scientist, still wearing her lab coat, earnestly questioning a colleague. The women stood near their seats, talking excitedly, trying to figure out why they had been called to Council so suddenly. Some Council members waved at Whit, delighted to see her. Some frowned with obvious disapproval. Everyone stared at Amelia.

Zoe placed her hand on the entry panel of the circular table, causing a section of table to slide away, allowing her to cross over to the other side of the council table. Arrogantly, she strode over to stand before the Leader's chair. The small warrior placed her fists on her hips, looking tough and self-righteous.

Several artisans rushed in, as ever, late. From her post as sentry near the main door, Nakotah caught Whit's eye and nodded encouragement.

Lilith came in last, clad in a well-cut white jumpsuit, with Branwen walking alongside, whispering in her ear.

Whit noted the white in Lilith's hair, the additional lines on the wisewoman's face. The blue eyes sparkled with warmth as they fell on Whit. Though in her sixties, Lilith was still a beautiful woman who carried herself with a noble air.

She remembered Lilith calling her "a rebellious scapegrace," when she had requested a tour of duty in Elysium. Lilith had warned her that the assignment required extreme self-discipline and an almost instinctual humility, which Whit clearly did not have.

Then, just before Whit was about to leave Lilith's chambers, full of disappointment, Lilith had reluctantly changed her mind. Sighing deeply, she said, "Cross the border, if you must, Major, but come back to us. Don't let this become an exercise in futility. You are too young to abandon all hope of happiness just yet."

"Council called to session," Lilith announced.

Whit came out of her reverie.

The buzzing room fell silent.

"What charges are brought and by whom?" Lilith asked formally in her musical voice.

"I, Captain Zoe Ference, bring charges of spying against this Elysian Castewoman, name unknown."

"It's Amelia!" Whit hollered, enraged all over again, wondering why Zoe was behaving in this bullish manner. *What are her motives?*

Zoe announced, "And against Major Tomyris Whitaker, I bring charges of resisting arrest and assisting an Elysian spy."

The women, shocked, all began to talk at once.

Lilith sternly called for order. The noise in the room subsiding, Nakotah opened the main door again. Whit glanced over and saw a voluptuous figure standing seductively in the doorway. *Cimbri.* For a moment, Whit couldn't breathe.

Then Nakotah let the huge oak door swing shut. With a sharp thump the wood smacked into Cimbri's curvaceous body. Cimbri cursed, Nakotah laughed, and Council members turned to see what they were missing in the doorway. Furious with herself for her dumbstruck reaction, Whit tore her eyes away and ignored the latecomer.

Zoe was talking all the while, listing charges that seemed more incredible with each sentence. "...due to this Spy," she droned on, "many of the cache computers on the northern route are now inoperative. Furthermore, the Elysian attacked me without provocation..."

And then, Amelia slumped against Whit, slid to the floor.

Lilith signalled Cimbri.

Whit bent down, clumsy with fatigue and the awkwardness of the chains restraining her. Someone knelt beside her. A dark brown hand smoothed across Amelia's brow.

Whit drew in a sharp breath, completely undone by Cimbri's nearness, instantly rocked by the mild scent of her skin.

Cimbri looked into her eyes. "This Elysian is blazing with fever. Why?"

Dry-mouthed, Whit answered, "Sword cut. Two months ago. I did all I could..."

Cimbri searched her eyes, as if she heard something beyond a health report. Abruptly, the healer gestured to the warriors in Zoe's patrol. Nakotah and her friend, Griffin, hurried over to them.

"Help me take her to the clinic," Cimbri said, with a simple authority, then added with a glance at the shackles, "And get those barbaric things off of her."

Nakotah tapped her personal security code into the digital computer on the wrist cuff, releasing all four metal bands. The warriors lifted Amelia carefully. Cimbri led them out of the Cedar House and Whit was left alone before the Council.

Lilith waited and the women gradually quieted. All eyes riveted on Whit.

"You have demanded Council, Major Whitaker," Lilith said kindly, steering events back to procedure. "You have been granted hearing. State your case, please."

Whit stood up. She told the tale from the beginning, when the Elysian jet had predictably malfunctioned and crashed into Baubo's field, to the end, when Amelia had been violently chained. Her voice went hoarse somewhere in the middle, but she pressed on, telling them about the woman who had crossed the Border with her, about the courage and intellect she had learned to value.

"When we started this journey," Whit finished, "I thought that my society was very much superior to hers. Now I am not so sure."

"You malign your country?" Zoe accused.

"I malign individuals like you!" Whit answered, irate, her gray eyes searing into Zoe. "You were brutal! I told you she had been stabbed by a Reg, yet you still struck her after she had given up, after the shackles went on."

"She is an Elysian. Why do you concern yourself?" Zoe folded her arms across her chest, bored, uninterested in Amelia's humanity.

"You behaved like a Regulator."

The Council stirred with discomfort.

Lilith asked, "Major Whitaker, did you see Baubo?"

"Amelia showed me her stones."

Lilith sat back, obviously grieved by this news.

Zoe said, "The Elysian is lying. Baubo was probably seized and this young Castewoman substituted. The Elysians have probably discovered the northern Bordergate by now."

Lilith replied reprovingly, "Conjecture, Captain." She folded her delicate hands together on the table. "We must have the Elysian's story to know more."

"Ask her accomplice," Zoe said, contemptuous. "They spent over two months together, alone in the Wilderness. They no doubt know each other very well. They are probably lovers!"

I'm going to strangle her! Whit thought. Instead she took a deep breath and strove for a professional demeanor. "I have told Amelia relatively nothing about myself, Freeland or the colony of Artemis. My secrecy," Whit searched for the right word, "irritated her. In return, she has told me almost nothing about herself. I only know she cared for Baubo. I saw it on her face when she showed me the burial place."

Lilith again took control of the Council hearing. "We shall wait until this Amelia can speak for herself." She turned to Zoe. "Captain Ference, you have been accused of abusing your prisoner. Do you wish to offer justification?"

Zoe made an exasperated gesture. "All *I* did was arrest an enemy."

Clearly annoyed, Lilith asked if anyone had anything more to say.

The hall remained silent.

Lilith said calmly, "The Council shall now vote. Enter into the computer one of these two options. One, charges against Major Whitaker shall be dismissed. Or two, charges shall be investigated and we shall proceed with a trial."

The Council members bent over the table, tapping their verdicts into the small, quartz crystal plates before each of them.

Lilith stated, for the record, that she would require daily reports from Cimbri concerning the health of the Elysian, Amelia. Then, casually turning to Zoe, Lilith told her to turn in her sedation gun and warrior badge, pending the outcome of an investigation into her conduct.

Astonished, Zoe stared angrily at Lilith.

Lilith instructed the warriors present who had been on Zoe's patrol to file a deposition about what they had witnessed.

Zoe sent the warriors an uneasy glance.

After consulting the computer tabulations of the Council vote, Lilith announced, "Charges against Major Whitaker are unanimously dismissed."

Zoe swore, ripping her badge from her uniform. When she flung her stun gun on the table, Lilith raised an eyebrow, then continued, "Charges against the Elysian, Amelia, shall be reviewed when she is well enough to meet with Council. Until such time, I invoke the Leader's Ward Statute. She will reside with me."

Zoe swore again.

Lilith referred to the papers before her, "The Articles of Artemis state, 'The Leader's Ward shall enjoy the freedoms and privileges of a born Freelander, until her citizenship is granted or denied in a clearance hearing before the Colony Council.'"

The Council made an approving noise.

"What?" Zoe sputtered. "The shackle law..."

Lilith finished, "Does not apply."

"She's an Aryan! A psychopath," Zoe protested futilely. "You can't turn her loose!"

Lilith continued, "The investigation into alleged abuse of a prisoner by Captain Zoe Ference will be coordinated by Co-leader Branwen Evans. Thank you, Council. Good night."

A gleeful roar filled the room.

Whit sat down in her chair abruptly, relieved at the outcome, and instantly aware of how tired and hungry and dirty she felt. Branwen was beside her, releasing the shackles.

Lilith, looking pleased, took Whit's free hand, remarking wryly, "A very dramatic return to Artemis."

Whit stood up and hugged her hard.

— 5 —

Council members, elated at Whit's return, thronged around her. Hands reached out to touch her, voices spoke to her in a never-ending stream of admiration and excitement.

"No one has ever downloaded data from Reg Dispatch!" one woman yelled excitedly, sidling up close to Whit.

"When Lilith told us that you had raided their mainframe, stealing years of reports, we just couldn't believe it," an elder agreed.

A robust aircraft mechanic clapped Whit on the back. "I hear you beamed back so much material that Co-leader Evans will be busy indexing it for months!"

"That was the ingenious part!" an executive enthused, "Utilizing the telecommunications satellites still orbiting the earth!"

Feeling slightly overwhelmed, and more than a little embarrassed by the praise, Whit began excusing herself.

Lilith narrowed her blue eyes, and showing concern, asked, "Where are you off to?"

"Amelia..." Whit replied, too tired to explain the need she felt. *I have to be sure Amelia is all right.* She ended up motioning lamely at the door.

"She's being cared for by the best healer in the colony. You must be hungry and you certainly look like you need a bath."

Whit grinned, blushing, but insisted, "She is my responsibility." Running her fingers through her hair, she shrugged her shoulders, while looking warmly at Lilith. Lilith, who had taken care of Whit since her mother had died.

"Oh, is she, now?" Lilith commented.

Whit again shrugged and began moving through the crowd. Lilith, though uninvited, went along with her. Once they were outside, away from the others, Lilith remarked, "Was the insinuation Zoe tried to make accurate, then? Are you lovers?"

Startled, Whit replied, "No! I am only fond of her."

They walked down the street together, Lilith, a founding Mother of Artemis, hurrying to keep up with Whit's long stride.

Lilith observed with a mother's eye, "You have grown thin, daughter. Your clothes hang on you. You are so travelworn your britches have holes and your eyes blink with exhaustion. And despite all this you can only think of one thing..."

Whit, not certain what to say, stayed silent.

"I was in love, once," Lilith finally said. "In all my sixty years, only once."

Just ahead, Whit saw Cimbri's clinic, looking larger and more prosperous than the small room she had known two years ago.

"Someone broke my heart," Lilith went on, "and I never let myself love again."

Sensing a lesson was being given, Whit frowned.

"I was afraid and too foolish to admit it," Lilith continued.

Whit stopped walking and faced her with hands on hips. "Are you making a comparison, Lilith?" she demanded, with a hint of a smile.

"Do you find a comparison, daughter?"

Whit hesitated, then growled, "I was one of many fishes in Cimbri's net. I hated it. I felt insignificant."

Lilith laughed softly. "And so you went after Branwen, the woman who refused all offers."

"Yes," Whit answered, annoyed.

"And when the ice-maiden finally melted with your touch, you felt strangely compelled to volunteer for a dangerous assignment, a remote posting we normally don't even fill any more. You risked your life. Don't you think that was strange?" she asked, throwing a piercing glance at Whit.

"I am over that," Whit said, lowering her voice.

"And over Cimbri?"

Whit did not reply, instead marching into the clinic.

Lilith acknowledged two warriors as they passed. Then, noting that they were not alone in the clinic, Lilith mused, "Your Elysian friend seems to be well-liked."

Whit noticed Nakotah and Griffin, off-duty now but still leaning against the wall, waiting for news of Amelia's condition. The competition was obviously lining up to be noticed.

Whit wanted to shake Lilith out of her stubborn short-sightedness.

*****

When Whit heard the electronic hum of the office door sliding open, she snapped awake. Before her, Cimbri was bustling over some charts, unbelievably ravishing in baggy, pale-green surgical scrubs.

Oh Mother, help me be strong.

Cimbri looked up in surprise, commenting, "What are you doing here so late? It's past midnight."

Lilith said, "Major Whitaker insisted on being here. You know how loyal she is," Lilith kept her tone light, but Whit grasped the intentional dig at Cimbri.

Cimbri sat down at the computer, back turned to them. "You're here about the report?"

"Yes," Whit managed.

Cimbri looked amused, then went professional. "The cut was badly infected."

Looking at the monitor, Cimbri's fingers danced over the keyboard. Whit could feel the memory of those fingers moving over her and only half heard what she said.

"That sword sliced right to the bone," Cimbri embellished, "and I went even deeper. The Elysian is anemic and physically ravaged from the long corruption of the wound. I can't imagine how she managed to walk so far with a wound this profound. She must have driven you mad with complaining, Whit."

"No. As a matter of fact, she never said a word."

Lilith raised an eyebrow. "Elysian training?"

Turning to Lilith, Cimbri continued, "A night in containment might have finished her—especially in Zoe's custody. The caustic Captain has a personality disorder, Lilith. She shouldn't be in a position of authority."

Lilith pondered a moment, carefully replied, "Hopefully, Whit has provided the Council with a means to de-throne our little dictator."

Returning to the monitor, Cimbri focused on completing the on-screen medical charts. About once every two minutes, she turned and casually cast a hungry gaze at Whit.

Studying the curving lines beneath Cimbri's surgical scrubs, Whit remembered how that sienna-colored body had felt pressed against her. Each time Cimbri looked at her, Whit felt her defenses collapse a little more.

"What about her AGH status?" Whit asked at last. "Is she too ill to endure a vaccination attempt?"

Lilith peered at her, somewhat surprised at the question.

Cimbri, also surprised at Whit's question, said, "There is no AGH. I thought you knew."

"What?" The word slid out of Whit.

"I saw the wrist tatoo during the Vital Signs check, of course, and then ran the blood tests. Our Elysian is AGH negative."

"You must be mistaken," Whit insisted. "There were lesions...Karposi's sarcoma..."

Cimbri looked provoked. "What lesions? I ran the test three times, standard procedure. She's clean. In fact, she's a virgin."

Whit bridled. "There was no reason to do a *pelvic* exam! Was there?!"

"Indeed?" Cimbri snapped. "Don't tell me how to practice medicine, Major."

Whit noticed Lilith staring at her, eyebrows raised. "It's just that Amelia is...incredibly modest."

Cimbri smiled, as if in victory. "You mean you haven't..."

Whit burst out, "I mean she's not like you! She can manage to interact with a woman without..."

"Careful, Tomyris," Lilith whispered, with a twinkle in her eyes.

Whit sat rigid, fuming, gripping her knees with her hands. Cimbri swiveled the chair back to the computer, without a word.

Lilith observed the two of them. After a few moments, she softly asked, "Whit, would you like to stay with me until things with Amelia are settled? Your place in the country will cause you a lot of traveling back and forth, otherwise."

Before Whit could answer, Cimbri said quickly, "Oh, Whit, stay with me. We have so much to talk about."

Whit, looking from one to the other and noting their sincerity, replied quietly, "I'm bunking in the warriors' barracks, until Amelia goes before the Council." She stood up, squared her tired, broad shoulders, and abruptly strode out of the office.

Lilith trailed after her, shaking her head.

*****

Who's screaming? Amelia heard it echoing, bouncing off walls. Then in a rush of comprehension, she knew that it was she who was screaming.

She found herself sitting up. Someone was holding her, trying to comfort her. Amelia panicked, pushed the stranger away.

A lovely woman stepped back. The hands and face were a dark, smooth brown, like river water after a rainstorm. The black hair was neatly held in many small braids, tied back in a ribbon that matched the red of the skin-tight suit the woman wore. Deep, brown eyes glimmered with kindness.

Amelia surveyed her, frightened, bewildered. "Where's Whit?" she mumbled.

"She'll be here, soon," the woman comforted. "Go back to sleep, Amelia."

She saw several other beds in the room, odd-looking machines, cabinets full of containers and instruments. The brown woman next to her moved closer and something pricked Amelia's arm. She pulled away, trying to get her legs out from under the light covers. Her right arm wouldn't work at all and when she looked at it to determine why, she found that she was wearing no clothes. Bandages criss-crossed her chest and shoulder, her pale breast poked through the arrangement like a small, fleshy pyramid.

The consternation she felt came out in a soft, ridiculous giggle. Her eyes closed slowly, once, twice, and then she was in someone's arms, being lowered into oblivion.

*****

When Amelia opened her eyes again, she saw Whit standing at the foot of the bed, talking earnestly with the dark-skinned stranger. Feeling groggy and sick, unable to move, Amelia lay listening. It took several minutes before she could decipher what they were saying.

Whit's husky voice had the same effect as that soothing hand easing through her hair. "But the Regs are never wrong," she was saying. "And even though the marks are gone now, there *were* lesions when I first met her."

"I'm telling you, she's clean, no trace of the AIDS Genital Herpes mutation. In fact, I lasered the tatoo off the other day. The skin on her wrist will soon heal, like the rest of her."

The sound of the voices became too low to hear. Amelia floated on the edge of sleep, the voices barely intruding.

"I only said she was appealing," someone complained.

"She's an innocent, Cimbri. Let her make her own discoveries."

A velvet laugh rang out. "You mean let her discover *you*." Amelia barely lifted her eyelids.

Whit was frowning, raking her hand through her thick, black hair. "There is something unusual about this woman."

Cimbri teased. "Since she has been in my clinic, you have visited every day. Mother, when we were lovers you were never over here as much!"

"You were too busy with your other admirers to know if I was here or not!" Whit flung back.

Cimbri, smiling with dark, piercing eyes, touched Whit's arm and murmured, "So passionate. How I loved your passion, Whit."

Whit quickly crossed the room. Cimbri moved after her. Near the infirmary door Cimbri stopped and let Whit pass through the portal alone.

Amelia blinked groggily, watching the proud shoulders sag. Cimbri turned around, came closer. Amelia pretended to be asleep.

In seconds the pretense was reality.

*****

Each day, Whit came to the clinic and sat beside Amelia's bed. The visits became Amelia's only link to anything familiar. She was in a strange place, among strange women and she felt extremely vulnerable. Terrifying dreams of Regulators and roaring fires and chains on her hands and feet plagued her. The apprehension only seemed to subside when Whit's handsome, friendly face loomed above her.

She was the same stalwart, curt companion Amelia had come to appreciate during their long trek across the Freelandian Wilderness. The first day Amelia could stay awake long enough to talk, Whit gently teased her about the punches she had given Zoe. Amelia was seriously weakened from the infected shoulder wound and fuzzy-headed from the medicines, so she didn't notice, then, the change in Whit when Cimbri was in the room.

The conversation she had overheard seemed vague and dreamlike, the intimation of a past romance between Whit and Cimbri seemed to have no concrete basis. In front of her, they interacted in a professional exchange of short sentences and betrayed no deep emotion.

But gradually, as Amelia grew stronger and her mind became clearer, she noticed that Whit went silent, became tense and withdrawn whenever Cimbri came to her bedside. She also noticed that Cimbri tried to ignore Whit, or sent exasperated looks at her, as if Whit were a child behaving badly. There was an energy in the room when Whit and Cimbri were there together, an energy that was palpable, an energy that defied being ignored, yet no one spoke of it.

At night, alone in the infirmary, Amelia wondered why she was so interested in this tension between Whit and Cimbri.

*.,.***

Cimbri fastened a soft belt around the waist of Amelia's white, terry cloth robe. With a gentle push, the dark-skinned woman urged Amelia to take her supporting hand to help her from the bed. Cimbri gripped the handles on the back of the belt.

"I won't fall," Amelia grumbled, though she concentrated carefully on balancing from one step to the next.

"You've been in bed for nearly two weeks now, and stupefied from the painkillers most of the time," replied the healer, "so don't be cocky."

"I made it across the Wilderness," Amelia muttered.

After one successful escorted walk down the length of the room, she began to feel steadier. Her eyes, finally clear after days of sleep, cast about, fascinated by closer views of things she had seen from her bed. On this side of the room, cabinets with glass fronts rose above a long, metal counter. Complex-looking medical equipment lined the shiny counter surface, ready for use.

In her rambling conversations with the healer, it had become clear to Amelia that Cimbri knew far more about the healing properties of plants than Baubo herself. Yet the cabinets were filled with jars of powder, not dried weeds or herbs.

What a bizarre place this is, Amelia thought.

They reached a blank, pastel, pink wall and turned to make the walk back. She noticed Cimbri watching her and felt self-conscious.

"Would you like me to explain about what you see?" Cimbri inquired.

Surprised, Amelia nodded eagerly. *At last, information! Whit never tells me anything.* Aloud she said, "Where are your medicine-plants?"

"A chemist processes the plants and makes these powders for me. I could do it myself, but it's time-consuming. I'd rather have more time to play." There was heat in the look Cimbri sent her.

Amelia nearly lost her balance.

Cimbri checked the drift to the right with a small tug on the belt.

Anxious for a distraction, Amelia gestured at the odd-looking box that rolled on wheels. Thin, stainless steel, pen-like instruments were mounted on each side. Cimbri called it a surgical laser, and told her she had used the tiny beams of light in certain operations.

"But light has no substance. How can it be used as a tool?" Amelia wondered.

"Light is a form of energy. It has many different bands in its spectrum and these different bands provide different sources of energy," Cimbri explained. "For example, in another part of this building I have a reproductive lab where parthenogenic procedures are..."

Amelia interrupted, "Parthano what?"

The broad smile on Cimbri's face was enchanting. They began walking again as Cimbri elaborated. "We do not need men in Artemis, nor do we want them. When a woman decides to have a child, she goes to see a healer who specializes in reproduction.

"The procedure is really quite simple, Amelia. First we retrieve an egg during the woman's ovulatory cycle. Then we get a donor's egg, preferably one from a woman who wants to share in the parenting of the child that will be produced. But children are considered precious, here, and we have many single parent households, too."

Nodding, Amelia concentrated on making the turn. Cimbri was gesturing with her hand, warming to her topic, and not quite noticing that Amelia was weakening.

"In the lab, the healer performs a procedure called parthenogenesis. We use a very fine laser beam to slice open one ovum or egg shell. Then with the use of an electron microscope, the chromosomes of the donor's ovum are carefully removed and placed in the ovum or egg cell of the mother to be. The fertilized egg is placed in a test tube and allowed to become mitotic..."

"Wait, wait," Amelia insisted, completely baffled. *"No men?"*

"And sometimes no physical pregnancy," Cimbri informed her, laughing. "Some women never have the fertilized egg implanted in their uterine wall. Instead, they elect to have the embryo/fetus mature in a perfectly supportive artificial womb for nine months, at the Delphi clinic. In that way, we free the mothers to continue with their work—which, more than likely, is a vital contribution to the welfare of the colony."

Amelia's eyes grew huge with wonder at what she was hearing.

Cimbri continued, "Most women use their life-partner as donor, but any woman who is prominent in the community ends up getting requests for eggs." Cimbri made a rueful laugh. "The women are always after Whit."

Amelia exclaimed, "Whit has children?"

"No," Cimbri laughed. "She's a traditionalist and thinks her off-spring should be in her family, where she can be an active participant in the child's growth. She's compulsively responsible,

I think. It hurts the community to have restricted access to a strong gene pool."

Amelia said nothing, but decided that she liked Whit all the more for what Cimbri saw as a failing. She stumbled on the next turn and was promptly steered back to bed.

*****

A week later, Amelia was walking alone, slowly lifting her sore arm and then bringing it back to her side. She reached the pink wall and turned around again. Cimbri called this "physical therapy;" Amelia called it boring.

I can't wait to see what's outside this clinic.

Most wondrous of all the clinic equipment, was the small, hand held MRI scanner that looked deep inside her shoulder and bone, and produced three dimensional color imaging, without Amelia even feeling it. Cimbri had showed her the recorded scan tapes of the wound, from the first night on; the ugly mess that had glowed an angry red and white on the first scanning video, had gradually healed. Only the strange, fibrous look remained, now. Cimbri said the fiber was scar tissue and told her she needed to move the shoulder in order to stretch and soften it.

After three weeks of taking various medicines and lying in bed, the sutures had magically disappeared into her skin and she was at last being allowed to walk whenever she wanted. *But when can I get out of here? And what will my life be like?* she wondered.

*****

Three days later, Cimbri slipped the blue sling off Amelia's arm and shoulder and peeled off a thin, gauze bandage. Embarrassed, Amelia subtly tried to pull her clinic shirt back over her bare chest.

"Why do you blush? You should be proud of your breasts," Cimbri admonished.

Amelia felt her face turn scarlet.

After examining her shoulder, poking and prodding, Cimbri helped Amelia dress herself. Amelia noticed that she wasn't given one of the robes Whit had brought for her several weeks ago. Instead, there were dark blue trousers and ankle boots and a turquoise shirt. They were beautiful, soft, cotton clothes and Amelia was delighted.

While Amelia sat on the edge of the bed, struggling with the buttons of the shirt, Cimbri typed a chart notation into the medex-computer. Amelia secured the last button and looked up, pleased with herself. Cimbri smiled, obviously happy about the buttons, too.

She said, "I think you're well enough to leave."

Amelia wasn't sure if this was good news or not. As anxious as she had been to leave and see the city beyond these clinic walls, she was also slightly fearful. She had grown accustomed to this refuge, to the caring attentions of Whit and Cimbri.

"Your wound is healing nicely," Cimbri continued, "but you are still weak. In other words, you are not to roam Freeland like a curious coyote."

Amelia noticed that Cimbri was inspecting her, her expression subtly different.

Then, Cimbri announced, "You have been invited to stay with Lilith, our Leader. This is a great honor and I am sure it has something to do with saving Whit from that filthy Reg. Zoe is having a fit about the breach of security, but we sensible citizens of Artemis are all satisfied."

Thinking of Zoe's vexation made Amelia laugh.

Cimbri moved a little closer to her, saying, "You're quite pretty when you smile."

Amelia sobered immediately. Cimbri was gazing at her in that suggestive way. It was too reminiscent of the Regulators. Cimbri said quietly, "Whit said you were a serf, operating a farm. According to Elysian law that means you have AGH. Yet, I found no evidence of infection in you."

Amelia felt held by the deep brown eyes, the depths that seemed so soft, so compelling. Hesitantly, she clarified, "Baubo faked the disease to keep me out of the Breeding Pens. I was on my way there, once...I think."

"You think?" Cimbri asked, shifting closer.

"I don't remember much before Baubo found me."

Cimbri was disconcertingly close. Amelia opened her mouth to comment on it when Cimbri's lips landed on her own. Cimbri's arms went smoothly and firmly around her.

The slow, sweet pressure on her mouth seemed to reach down into her deepest flesh, tugging awake odd, fiery sensations. Cimbri gently, insistently pulled her closer. A spiraling need broke loose in Amelia. She lost whatever misgivings she had initially had and leaned into this marvelous surprise.

— 6 —

Whit came to the door and saw them through the glass. She touched the DNA plate. The door slid open with an audible hum, and Cimbri stepped away from Amelia, greeting Whit with a mischievous smile. Whit scowled at her and then she studied Amelia.

The round brown eyes remained on Cimbri. Amelia looked breathless, astonished, flushed with excitement. She did not look displeased.

Whit was disgusted, then furious, and snarled at Cimbri, "Lilith sent me for her."

Cimbri gave Amelia a parting smile and said, "Tomorrow I will come to see you. About the wound."

Amelia nodded, mute.

Whit took Amelia's elbow and guided her out of the room. Upon emerging from the clinic into bright sunlight, Amelia stopped and put her hand up, shadowing her eyes against the glare.

"You're making us late," Whit snapped.

Tense, indignant, Amelia demanded, "Have I done something wrong—broken some law again?"

Whit realized the question was serious. Her rage diffused a bit. "You did nothing wrong," she grumbled. "Cimbri...likes to make me angry."

The round brown eyes shifted, looked past her.

Whit turned and saw Zoe approaching. The slicked, brown hair was standing straight up. *She looks like a rooster*, Whit thought, and nearly laughed. Then Whit noticed a set of shackles swinging from Zoe's empty gun belt.

"Our esteemed Leader chooses to harbor an Elysian. My mother shrieks in her mountain grave," Zoe said, glaring at Amelia.

"I'm in no mood for you, Zoe," Whit warned.

Coming nearer, Zoe crooned, "I know what you're in the mood for, Major." She reached out and stroked Amelia's cheek.

Amelia recoiled from her touch, dropping down into a defensive crouch. Whit recognized the reaction. It was a Freeland warrior's siance, the prelude to combat.

Zoe looked shocked, then a murderous gleam flickered in her green eyes. "What else have they taught you, Spy?"

Whit suddenly knew she had to keep these two apart. She took the Castewoman's forearm again. "Come on, Amelia. Lilith is waiting."

They left Zoe behind and moved along the street. Whit fell silent, feeling unsettled by the increasing mystery of this woman by her side.

*****

No men. Amelia noted the absence, remembering Cimbri's casual reference to the fact. In the clinic it had stirred her imagination, but out here, on the street, in broad daylight, it was...well, it felt completely natural.

As she and Whit walked, women passed them. Old women, young women, girl children, all moving along, full of purpose and apparently in good health. No downcast eyes, no meek silence, no female training in evidence. They were robustly loud, they were brazenly eyeing her and Whit. It began to be a little overwhelming.

With delight, Amelia studied the buildings they were passing. Stone, brick, wood, and materials she had no name for, all constructed in sturdy, graceful lines. Intricate woodwork and bright paint adorned the walls. There were large, open windows; colorful flowering plants rested on the sills. All the houses seemed to stop at three stories high, though some were lower. Some homes had porches that wrapped around the low or high part of the house. On one high deck, Amelia noticed a woman lounging against a railing, staring down hard at Whit.

Amelia hurried to catch up with the determined, dark-haired woman striding before her. Whit was wearing a loose, gray tunic that emphasized her shoulders and set off her eyes. She looked dynamic and rugged and...

Regal. Amelia concluded. *She looks like she could lead all of Freeland.*

"Are the other city-colonies like this?" Amelia asked.

"Pretty much," Whit answered. "In the southwest, the Mexican influence is stronger. There's a preference for adobe down there."

"No, I mean...are they cities of women?"

"Oh," Whit laughed. "Are they *lesbian.* Yes, although there are two colonies that have a minority male population and are fairly hetero. And then there's Harvey, which is south of here, on Harvey Bay—old California territory. Harvey is almost entirely gay male."

Amelia's eyes grew large with astonishment as she listened to Whit, but said nothing. A bicyclist coasted by them, nearly hitting Amelia, whose eyes were roaming everywhere in wonder. Whit reached out and drew her closer. The broad street had emptied into a bustling open market area, packed with women and booths and all manner of tempting goods.

"This is the marketplace," Whit said, raising her voice above the crowd noise. "Stay close beside me."

Whit headed into the throngs of women and Amelia followed. Bodies brushed against Amelia, faces smiled at her. She heard voices asking, "Who is that?"

Return to Isis

Near the heart of the square the market became a virtual kaleidoscope of sound, smell and color. They passed a group of musicians and Amelia stopped, enthralled, until Whit came back and pulled her away. She stared at the flipping acrobats, the willowy dancers. Before the various wooden stalls she saw carpenters, weavers, tailors, cobblers—all displaying their wares. When they saw her gaze lingering, they called to her, held up the object that had caught her eye.

The press of bodies became very thick. Women walked by carrying plates of steaming food. And then, seduced by the savory smells from the cookpots, she wandered from Whit's side. She came to a space beyond the small shops, where the food was obviously prepared for sale. Cast iron kettles sat on stone ovens. Bowls and utensils, freshly washed, sat beside huge, steel tubs of dishwater.

She turned and found herself standing before a broad table displaying a variety of bread. She stood there, transfixed, her mouth watering. Amelia, who had spent her days in Elysium constantly hungry, had never before she seen such abundance: stacks and stacks of fresh, golden loaves—and all of it unguarded. She suddenly felt as if she couldn't breathe, as if the earth were tilting out from under her.

Whit appeared at her side, studied the bread for a moment. The gray eyes met her own. "I know," Whit stated solemnly, the husky voice full of feeling. And then Whit took her hand and led her back into the crush of bodies.

As they were emerging on the other side of the square, they accidentally encountered Nakotah by a booth of scarves. The tall Native American draped one around Amelia's neck, inviting her to come share a meal. Whit stood aside, looking fretful and impatient, until she heard the refusal.

Amelia fell in step behind Whit, who had gone silent and stony again. They were walking uphill, toward an imposing granite house that sat alone on the crest.

What's wrong with her? Amelia wondered.

Ever since they had met that band of warriors on the mountainside, Whit had been so moody. And just what was going on between Whit and Cimbri? They obviously had shared something...something that still glowed between them like an ember in a neglected hearth fire. Yet, they only seemed to torment each other.

As Amelia followed Whit through the marketplace, she recalled Baubo's tales of a tribe of warrior women who looked to one another for everything, including love. Strangely, it did not shock her to see the open intimacy between women here, though Whit had watched her when public displays occurred, as if it should. The women embracing in the marketplace had intrigued her. The way Nakotah had looped the scarf around her neck had made her feel...significant.

But why had Cimbri done that to her, touched lips like that? If Cimbri's eyes followed Whit so helplessly, why would Cimbri reach for anyone else? Amelia couldn't understand it.

And what about that hand slipping through her hair? What did it mean? Was she of interest to Whit, the way she was of interest to Nakotah? If so, why was Whit trying to mask whatever feelings she felt? Her friend had become a thorny briar patch.

Whit strode up to the huge, granite house, touched a small, shiny surface by the glass door and the door slid open.

"This is where you'll be living until you're granted clearance," Whit muttered, still looking vexed.

Amelia followed her into a sunlit hallway. There were glass walls. She could look right through the house and see women in loose, colorful clothing leaning over desks, sitting before computer units similar to the ones she had seen in Cimbri's office. A large map was mounted on a stone wall that marked the end of the building. Wooden book cases, also like Cimbri's, were positioned along the glass partitions.

She couldn't help noticing the vases of multi-colored, full-blossomed chrysanthemums that were displayed on various surfaces. Function and beauty seemed to go hand in hand in Artemis.

Everything looked efficient, well-made—and yet there was this extra touch, this stroke of decoration, to liven the scene.

Whit headed for the stairs at the intersection of two halls. The warrior was climbing upward two steps at a time, as Amelia was still looking back over her shoulder, stumbling on each stair.

At the top, Whit showed her into a chamber with solid, conventional, plaster walls. Amelia reached out and the touched the sunny, yellow paint, while Whit backed away, obviously intent on leaving her.

"I'll go get Lilith. You stay here. I want a word with her, so we may be a few minutes."

Amelia nodded, feeling like a child that Whit had grown tired of entertaining.

Whit left, shutting the door behind her.

Out of curiosity, Amelia went to the plate mounted in the wall. She touched it, hoping to make the door work as Whit had. The door did not move. And then Amelia realized that she was being contained here, just as she had been contained at Cimbri's clinic.

So, Zoe isn't the only one who doesn't trust me.

Amelia crossed the room to the immense window. She leaned against the plexiglass, trying to steady her nerve, trying to concentrate on the view. She was glad Whit had elected to have a private conversation with this leader they called Lilith. Amelia desperately needed time to re-orient her senses.

Beyond the window, lay the city of Artemis and beyond that, the deep blue of water. The Leader's House was two stories high and on a hill. Amelia was able to gaze down the wide and busy street, all the way to the marketplace.

I never dreamed it would be like this.

There were no skyscrapers, like the ones she had seen quite clearly from the heights of the old Chicago landfills. She could still remember Baubo, digging for plastic, slinging the refuse out of her way, remarking how odd it was that the high caste Elysians chose to live in concrete canyons.

Baubo had said that the high-rises in Seattle were giant tombs full of AGH victims; floor after floor of jumbled skeletons from the worst years of the plague, just after the Great Schism in 2010. She recalled Baubo saying that the Freelanders who had survived had abandoned the cities, had built new towns. The tall towers of Seattle finally became just one more western ghost town. Amelia came back to the present moment. Below her, bicyclists and pedestrians passed. She watched people sauntering along the shady, tree-lined street, stopping at the intersections for an occasional car or truck to roll by. It struck her that none of the women wore patched clothing. *What unbelievable wealth!*

Beginning to feel lightheaded, Amelia moved away from the window and wearily sat down on a long couch. Only out of the clinic an hour, she was already exhausted.

A pastoral scene had been painted on the chamber wall before her. Several large, rainbow-colored fish were leaping up a small waterfall. Baubo would call this a mural. Just one more of Baubo's far-fetched tales made splendidly real. A rush of tears blurred her vision.

The door hummed open and an elegantly dressed, dignified woman came toward her. Amelia jumped up and quickly rubbed her eyes with her shirt sleeve, afraid to be caught crying.

The woman stopped a few feet away, saying, "People are allowed to shed tears in Freeland. In fact, you'll probably have an easier time understanding our customs if you keep in mind one rule: do not intentionally cause anyone harm."

Amelia nodded. The crisp blue eyes seemed to penetrate her, reading her character, drawing conclusions.

"I am Lilith. Please be seated." The woman gestured toward a chair. "We have much to discuss."

Amelia obediently sank into the plush arm chair that seemed sculpted to the shape of a woman's body. The arm supports came up beneath her elbows like wings. Amelia grimaced as she raised her wounded shoulder.

Lilith moved behind a nearby table, studying the glassy surface as if she were reading something there.

"You must be very tired," Lilith commented.

Amelia answered, "A little."

Lilith looked at her again, the eyes just as piercing. "I have some questions that require answers."

Amelia took a deep breath. The woman's tone was warm and persuasive, yet the words reminded her of something, something awful. She had no memory to draw upon, only unquenchable, intuitive emotion. A niggling panic stirred at the bottom of her spine.

Lilith was staring at the table surface again. "How old are you, Amelia?"

Amelia replied, "Twenty-five."

The blue eyes flashed up at her. "And you were gotten at which Breeding Pen?"

"Chicago."

Lilith's eyebrows came down, betraying how perturbed she was.

Tense with anxiety, Amelia swallowed hard.

"Why are you so frightened, Amelia?" Lilith entreated softly. "Are you telling me the truth?"

Amelia gripped the chair and realized her palms were wet with perspiration. She stammered, "I...don't know my age or where I was gotten. I have no memory of...before Baubo. I have dreams, sometimes, that seem real. Baubo said the dreams are rooted in truth, but most of the time they make no sense to me."

Lilith studied her. "How did you know Baubo?"

"She found me, she said. I lived with her. We fed the land and the land fed us." Amelia relaxed a little, remembering the contentment of working beside Baubo in the fields.

"How long did you live with her?"

"Ten autumn harvests. Last winter the coughing sickness filled her lungs and I couldn't get permission for the medicine. They said she was too old." Tears of anger and grief flooded her, and out of habit, Amelia bent her head to hide them.

Lilith asked, "Did Baubo ever mention Freeland?"

Amelia mumbled, "I thought it was a fable."

Lilith paused. "How is it that you were classified a serf, when you did not have AGH?"

"Baubo made a paste from plants and we dabbed it on our skin. It gave us purplish-red welts, but it made both of us look like the other Farmers."

Lilith leaned forward, looking intrigued.

"Baubo told me I was damaged when she found me. She said I was so afraid of the Reg that tattooed me, that...I went into a trance...became dead with my eyes open." Amelia shook her head, baffled. "I don't remember those early years. I *do* know there was a time when I couldn't speak. Baubo was a healer—she helped me. She...she...loved me." Amelia stopped, a hard ache in her throat.

Lilith waited for her to recover, then asked gently, "Why did you allow Major Whitaker to think you both diseased and mentally impaired, when you were neither?"

"She...offended me."

Lilith turned away from her. The shoulders seemed to shake, then she said, "Explain how she offended you, please."

Amelia stated, "She acted as if she knew everything. She wouldn't listen to me when I tried to tell her...things. Since she had such pride in her knowledge, I let her think what she chose to think."

Lilith turned and looked down at the table. "And do you still find her offensive?"

Amelia said, "No. But she...angers me...I don't know the words for it."

"Does Cimbri offend you?"

Surprised, Amelia realized Whit had told Lilith about that mouth-touching. "Not as much." And as the words escaped Amelia, several other realizations fell in place.

She knew, all at once, that despite that marvelous meeting of mouths earlier, she felt stirred by Whit far more deeply than she felt stirred by Cimbri. She also knew that Whit felt something for her, and yet didn't want to acknowledge it.

Lilith watched her. "How is it you fight so well? How is it you kept pace with Major Whitaker against large Regulators? And, according to all reports, you threw Captain Ference off with great ease."

Amelia sighed. "I don't know." She felt incredibly tired and these questions made her head ache.

Lilith paused for a moment, then took a different tack. "Do you use something special on your teeth?"

Teeth? Amelia thought. Had she heard right? She shook her head in bewilderment.

Lilith asked, "Is Amelia your real name?"

"Baubo used to call me Amelia Earhart. She said I would know what it meant one day."

The Leader stood stock still, amazed by that answer. The blue-eyed stare seemed to go straight through Amelia. She shifted uncomfortably.

Rubbing her right temple, the Leader continued the questioning. "Captain Ference explained to you the law about Elysians being shackled in our city. Why did you resist?"

The fear came again, freezing cold fear shooting up and down her spine, into her limbs. She was breathing fast, unable to answer. Again, she felt the metal cuffs on her ankles, on her wrists, heard the chains jingle.

"Amelia?" Lilith shouted after her, as she bolted from the room, taking the stairs in a series of bounds. Whit, who was sitting on a bench at the bottom of the staircase, jumped up, and moved in front of her, heading off the flight.

"Amelia, slow down." Whit caught her arms. "Amelia, what's wrong?"

Amelia slowed to a walk and then stopped, her breath coming in huffs.

Whit stood before her, her gray eyes full of concern. "What is it?"

Trailing behind Amelia, Lilith came to Amelia's side. "I'm sorry I upset you, child. What frightens you so?"

Amelia gasped for air. "Do you ever have dreams, bad ones, that seem to have happened or might happen, or..." she faltered, her voice breaking with exhaustion.

Lilith and Whit looked perplexed, then Whit said gently, "Dreams? Lilith was trying to prepare you for your meeting with the Council." Looking at Lilith, Whit added, "Perhaps we are trying for too much, too soon."

Branwen rushed down the hallway and waved some papers at Lilith. Wisely contemplating Whit and Amelia, the Leader instructed, "Please look after our visitor, Major," and then calmly walked off to manage the apparent crisis.

Amelia gripped her throbbing forehead.

Soothingly, Whit suggested, "Why don't you rest for a while?"

Amelia nodded.

Whit guided her by the elbow, leading her back up the stairs. They passed the room where she had been questioned by Lilith, passed several other doors and came to a sunny chamber at the end of the hall.

Amelia barely noticed the paintings on the walls, the statues of women, the graceful furniture. She only saw the bed. She felt Whit pull her boots off and cover her. She lay still, eyes closed for a long while. Then, just as she had almost given up hope, she felt Whit's hand glide through her hair.

Before drifting off, Amelia resolved that there was only one mouth she wanted to meet.

*****

A golden-haired woman stood next to her, instructing in a melodic voice. The woman positioned her hands, a child's hands, on the keyboard. The bells above them began to play, making a song, delighting them both.

She was suddenly outside of the building, gazing up at a white tower against a blue, blue sky. The silver bells of the carillon flashed in the sunlight. The woman stood next to her, much taller than she. A huge, glowing feeling radiated between them, an exquisite energy.

A series of images. A wooden door. A long hall. An emblem—a deep purple, six-pointed star with a dolphin in the center. The word *Delphi* inscribed below the jumping mammal. The golden-haired woman, equal in height, embracing her, leading her into a vast room that smelled of cedar.

A tumult of vision now. Regulators everywhere. Women fighting them, guns flashing. The tall, white bell tower. Screams, women's screams, terrifying screams. She was looking frantically for someone, someone she couldn't leave. She felt a blast in the back. She was down, numb, unable to move. The Regulator picked her up by the scruff of her tunic and he was roaring in victory.

Another blurring rush, then shocking pain. Her stomach, her ribs. She hurt so much she thought she was dying. A man's voice was shouting, "Burn the witch!" Someone yanked her head up.

And in flames before her, a woman was screaming; a woman with golden hair.

*****

Screaming, far away, bouncing off walls, ringing in her ears. Someone was shaking her.

"Amelia!"

Lilith was shaking her. Lilith was sitting beside her on the bed. Lilith's blue eyes were wide with alarm, fastened on her. Her voice was earnest. "What do you dream of?"

As usual, it was already fading from her—leaving her soaked in sweat, rigid with adrenaline. Amelia shook her head. A tremor raced through her body, shuddered into great jerking spasms.

Lilith gathered her close.

The shaking slowly subsided. And for the first time since she and Whit had begun spending their nights apart, Amelia finally felt safe.

— 7 —

Early the next morning, Whit approached the Leader's House. The first settlers had transported the dark, granite rocks here from the base of Mount Tahoma, nearly eighty years ago, right after the Border officially cleaved America in two. The complex scheme of vast windows and multiple floors had been an architectural struggle in those days of limited resources. Still, the main concept had been achieved. Artemis and Puget Sound could be seen from any room in the house, and on a clear day it was possible to see the snow-capped Olympics.

After touching her fingertips to the DNA plate by the front door, Whit strode upstairs, into Lilith's empty office and stood before the oak desk, puzzled. It wasn't like Lilith to leave her duties so early in the day. Lilith was a virtual drudge, often laboring in this room far into the night.

Branwen brushed by her and placed a box of molecular memory disks next to the computer. "Lilith's down in the kitchen," Branwen said, "with your new friend."

There seemed to be something arch in the way Branwen delivered the words, but Whit ignored it. She was subtly twisting her head, trying to read the reference title on the box. The name, "Isis," had caught Whit's eye.

"I hear you're seeing quite a lot of her," Branwen said, her eyes keen with interest.

Whit pushed her hands into her trouser pockets. *Sweet Mother, how the women of Artemis love to gossip!* "I missed Lilith," she evaded.

"You know I don't mean Lilith. What's the little savage like?"

"Amelia's no savage!" Whit snapped, then muttered, "What a thing to say."

"You have no idea what's being said," Branwen returned, the blue eyes growing fierce.

Whit scowled back, a little shocked. Branwen usually confined all her conversations to superficial pleasantries. This seeping acid had to spring from jealousy.

"Bran, did you have expectations of me?"

The woman gave a dismissive laugh, "You were a skilled lover, Major, but you got nowhere near my heart." Branwen swept her eyes over Whit as if she were taking her measure. Then she turned to the computer and began working.

Trying for civility, Whit glanced at the program on-screen. "Have you found anything interesting in the Reg Dispatch files I sent to Lilith?"

Branwen fixed her with an inscrutable, chilling smile. "Yes, as a matter of fact, I have."

Whit waited for some elaboration. Branwen completely ignored her. Puzzled, Whit took the hint and left.

She marched down the hall, descended the stairs.

Lilith saw Whit come through the kitchen portal and called laughingly, "Don't worry, I'm not the cook."

Amelia, up to her wrists in the brown dough she was kneading, smiled. Lilith's orange tabby cat weaved in and out of Amelia's legs, rubbing his head on her boots.

"I can't believe this wealth of food," Amelia said, almost shyly. "So much fruit and wheat..."

The over-sized shirt hung loosely on Amelia's smaller frame, but Whit still recognized her old, faded, blue workshirt. The clothing she had lent looked strangely different on Amelia. The front was snowy with flour, but that wasn't it. Open at the neck and exposing flesh, it was the collar that held her attention. Whit pulled her eyes away with effort.

Lilith patted an empty stool. "Join us. I'm telling Amelia about the way we farm, but, as you are a farmer, perhaps..."

Amelia repeated, "A Farmer?"

Whit suddenly remembered the first week of their journey. She had regularly insulted the woman about her work with the earth.

Amelia stared at her. "You knew...you knew about...bugs, erosion, no rain." She clenched the mound of dough, looking ready to throw it at Whit. "And you called me 'peasant.' "

"I was ridiculing myself, not you," Whit admitted. She, who usually never explained herself to anyone, was giving an explanation. A sideways glance revealed that Lilith looked astounded.

Amelia, however, looked unconvinced.

Whit swallowed, then pressed on. "When we were both hungry and hurt, you knew the wild plants for healing and food..." Whit finished rapidly, "You're no more a peasant than I am."

Amelia's eyes widened, then dropped. She fixed all her attention on the bread dough she was kneading.

Lilith seemed to realize that she was going to have to carry the conversation. Although no one had asked, she began explaining basic hydroponics in a soft, authoritative voice.

"...we use a specialized chemical solution for each particular type of food producing plant. The hothouses are built over woman-made bodies of fresh water. Fine nets are spread over the water, with several feet between each berth. The vegetables and fruit grow on these nets. We maneuver the roots, train them to funnel themselves into irrigating tubes that run along the length of net..."

Whit watched the dough being lifted and folded, the hands flexing rhythmically under a dusting of brown flour. She felt a strange contentment drift over her, the way she had felt each night during their trek through the Wilderness. She and Amelia hunkered near the camp fire, quietly preparing a meal, content in each other's company.

I'm falling in love with her, Whit thought.

She abruptly slid off the stool. "Here's my report."

Startled, Lilith accepted the small disc box Whit had yanked out of her waist pouch and thrust at her.

"Perfect therapy for your shoulder," a rich voice called. Cimbri sauntered into the kitchen, the sienna skin glowing, the white smile flashing. A subtle shade of orange tinged the suit tightly encasing her womanly body.

Whit felt weak.

"You look good," Cimbri stated, her eyes moving over Amelia in a manner Whit remembered all too well. "How do you feel?"

"Strong," Amelia answered. "I was just about to ask Whit to show me more of the city."

"Oh, Gaea," Cimbri laughed. "Whit will only drag you through the Agri-Science Center. Seed experiments, silo maintenance, soil depletion measurement. She's fascinated with those things—can you imagine? Such a peasant!"

Whit felt her face flaming, but Cimbri only flicked a glance at her, then fixed her eyes back on Amelia.

She wheedled, "Let me take you to the shops. The clothes Whit has lent you are far too big for you." Cimbri reached out and gripped a thick yellow strand of hair. "And your gorgeous hair needs shaping."

Embarrassed, Amelia ducked out from under the contact, stating firmly, "I'd like to see the seed experiments."

Whit watched the dough getting vigorously mashed. Was Amelia annoyed?

Happily, Lilith intervened, "You can do both. I'll bake your bread while Whit and Cimbri take you out. Finish up, Amelia, then join us in the main chamber."

Lilith motioned Whit and Cimbri to the door and they left Amelia in the kitchen behind them.

As soon as they were out of Amelia's hearing, Cimbri muttered, "*I* do not wish to see seed experiments!"

Lilith returned, "Then go to the shops, first, and leave Amelia with Whit, later."

Cimbri reviewed Whit. "Lilith, do you think it is wise for them to be seen together, alone? Woman already assume that they're lovers. Zoe is casting rumor everywhere."

Glowering, Whit headed for the street door.

"Whit, stay," Lilith commanded. "Since when do any of us allow Zoe to dictate what we do? The fact is, Amelia needs clothing and Cimbri is gifted with apparel. Amelia is interested in farming and you are a wonderful resource for that. You will both help her. And don't worry about the gossips."

Lilith led them upstairs. Behind her back, Cimbri and Whit regarded each other coldly, both of them peevish.

"I want you to understand," Lilith went on patiently, "that she has known little but deprivation and fear. Elysium is a rigid caste system and Amelia lived at the very bottom. She was classified as a diseased female serf, and she was routinely beaten, starved, terrorized. If Baubo had not fooled the Regs with her herb-paste trick, the woman would be a just another womb in some Breeding Pen."

Lilith strode into the main chamber, eyeing Whit. "I know you were there for two years, but as a Computer Tech you lived a relatively privileged life."

Whit conceded with a nod, wondering why Lilith was being so emphatic. "What did you find out from the interview yesterday?"

Lilith sealed the sliding door. "Not much. Amelia claims she has no memory of her life before living with Baubo. The chair sensors analyzed her physical responses as high in fear, fatigue and pain. An unusual reading, considering how cool she appears, but as an Elysian, she has been taught to internalize her discomfort. I believe she's hiding something, but she's still very likable."

Cimbri nodded, a small, private smile on her lips, but something in Whit got tight and anxious.

Lilith moved to her desk and plucked a molecular electron memory disk from the box marked *Isis*. "One of those nightmares Cimbri told us of occurred last night. From my bed chamber, at the far end of the hall, I heard the screams." Lilith shivered. "No one could pretend that emotion, my dears. Amelia remembers something. And the way Zoe is campaigning against granting her clearance, we must find out what it is."

For the first time, Lilith seemed to notice the bright day beyond the window. "Early October—a glorious time to explore our fair city. Off with you, both. A certain young woman longs to be out in the sunshine. She's probably in her room, getting ready."

Mildly exasperated about having to endure a shopping expedition, Whit walked silently behind Cimbri to Amelia's room at the back of the second floor. Cimbri stopped before the open chamber door and called.

Amelia came out of the bathroom, hurriedly tucking in a fresh shirt. "I had flour all over me," she explained.

Whit noted that her old, red tunic and buff trousers were baggy, yet charming on Amelia. Cimbri seemed to like the look, too, for she was staring.

Though a chair was right beside her, Amelia sat down on the floor to lace up her boots.

She's so Elysian, Whit thought, amused.

Gazing around the chamber, Whit decided that her old room looked much the same. Sunshine poured in the window, falling over the high mattress platform. The pine dresser and chest of drawers both glowed with a recent woodwax. On the dresser stood the small, bronze statue of Artemis the Archer. The walls were still covered with Whit's collection of Amazon heroines.

Scrambling to her feet, Amelia announced that she was ready. Cimbri promptly took Amelia's arm and led the way into the hall; Whit trailed behind them, annoyed.

Cimbri was obviously in her element as she danced Amelia through the garment shops, standing behind her, holding clothes against her, murmuring compliments about "shining hair," and "glorious legs."

To Whit, the entire process seemed like one long seduction. Just as she was ready to depart in a sulk, she noticed that Amelia was consistently leaning away when Cimbri came too close. Finally, Cimbri noticed it, too, and looked a little flustered about it.

Then, Amelia resisted all of the revealing, skin-tight outfits that Cimbri favored, and selected loose, soft, functional clothing similar to the garments Whit wore. She politely refused to let Cimbri purchase anything and instead bartered with the shop owners, arranging purchase orders for baskets she would weave or herbs she would gather.

At last, Whit thought, a woman Cimbri cannot rule. It seemed almost unbelievable, especially after the kiss she had watched Cimbri bestow in the infirmary. But did this mean that Amelia was unaffected by women? Was she hetero—responsive only to men?

At the last stop, an intimate but well-appointed haircutting shop, Amelia reluctantly gave in to Cimbri's urgings and plopped into a chair. There she sat, almost asleep, while the hair stylist and Cimbri worked on her. The result was a layered cut that tapered down to her shirt collar and complemented her face. Whit found herself staring at the shiny, golden mane, pleased. She felt something shifting deep within her, something that made her feel good for the first time in ages.

After what seemed like hours to Whit, they dropped the parcels they had accumulated at Lilith's house. Amelia looked tired, but stubbornly rebelled against Cimbri's orders to go upstairs and nap. Whit promised that their visit to the Agri-Science Center would be short. When Cimbri left them, she had an expression Whit had never seen on that lovely face. She looked perplexed, as if she had entered unfamiliar territory and didn't know what action to take.

Whit borrowed Lilith's sleek electrobile for the excursion to the Center. After asking several questions about the electric engine and then toying with the audio chip-player, Amelia settled back and looked out the passenger window hungrily. A new rock symphony played softly from the speakers. Whit began to feel dangerously romantic.

Remember what Cimbri did to you, she cautioned herself. *Do you honestly want to go through that hell again?*

All the same, Amelia's knee was tantalizingly close, the music was so full of feeling. Whit kept both hands on the steering wheel, restraining the impulse to caress that leg. Mercifully, they reached the Agri-Center quickly.

Whit parked the car and they crossed the vast, plush lawn that marked the start of the campus. As youngsters passed by carrying knapsacks, hurrying to classes, Whit found herself remembering her days as a student here.

They entered the Projects Building and toured the labs. Amelia asked one question after another about seeds and crop yields and insect control. Until then, it had never occurred to Whit that she knew a great deal about the grain fields that surrounded Artemis. The labs were built over the underground storage facility, so they went down and read the temperature controls and other monitors on the deep-set silos.

They passed an open hopper of corn and Amelia dipped both hands into the kernels. A grave awe in her eyes, she lifted the pellets, let them sift through her fingers like gold coins.

Soon afterward, they left the Projects Building and meandered across the green lawn. Without a word, Amelia sank down on the grass. Whit sat beside her, observing a struggle in the haunted brown eyes. Amelia glanced at her, shut her eyes and dropped onto her back. Whit waited.

She was certain Amelia was experiencing something akin to the severe culture shock she herself had endured two years ago, after entering Elysium. It was very, very hard to believe that Freeland and Elysium had once been the same country.

As a Computer Technician in Elysium, Whit had been given regular sustenance. Compared to Freelandian meals, Elysian food had been meager and lacking in variety, but she had still seen at least one reasonable portion of food and water each day. Then, gradually, she had heard the rumors of how things were for the others. She had discovered that while the New Order Reverends, the Procurators, the Tribunes, the Regs and the Computer Techs had enough for survival, no one else was as fortunate.

Merchants supposedly stole food from the trash cans of the highest caste, the Reverends. And mechanics required meals while completing a repair, thus turning any equipment breakdown into an endless affair. Farmers, the ones who provided the food, were allowed to keep little of what they grew for themselves.

She had heard the quietest whispers, about the seasonal Reg Raids on the farming villages, the privileged gleaning of harvests and disease-free girls. Only then did she understand.

The stresses that had caused Freeland to go forward, to develop as a nation and a people—had caused Elysium to regress. Elysium had become medieval, with feudal law and the reign of great and petty tyrants. The Border was more than a laser field; it was almost a symbolic break in time.

"Funny smell," Amelia mumbled, sitting up.

"Someone's smoking salmon, probably down by the Sound. Between the grain and the salmon, Gaea the Mother has given us an abundance in food."

Amelia nodded, squinting at the small, brick structure next to the glinting glass of the Projects Building.

"That's the American Museum," Whit responded.

The blank look in the brown eyes told Whit that it was time for a history lesson. She helped Amelia up. As they crossed the grass, Whit started telling Amelia about the past that had spawned both Elysium and Freeland.

"There was a virus called AIDS," Whit began. "For several decades after it was first discovered, AIDS existed in certain groups of people, but most of America was unaffected. Then, around the year 2000, the AIDS virus mutated and bonded with another virus called Genital Herpes. No one noticed it until about seven years later, when large numbers of heterosexuals came down with odd forms of pneumonia and reproductive tract cancers. By then, AGH was well on its way to becoming the worst plague since the Black Death of the Middle Ages. There was...a panic."

Whit ran a hand through her hair. Talking about this always upset her. "America once stretched from the Atlantic to the Pacific Oceans. Remember that map I used when we were crossing the Wilderness?"

A slight nod made the blonde hair shimmer in the sunlight.

"All of that was America. And more. There were two other states off the mainland."

Climbing the steps, they went inside the museum. Slowly, they passed exhibit after exhibit. The artifacts of the last century were poignant. A child's illustrated storybook. Photographs of supermarket aisles; row after row of processed food. A package of bubble gum. A can of diet soda.

In one video booth after another they watched films of crowded city streets, of cars bumper to bumper on highways, of factory smokestacks spewing dark, thick plumes of toxic smoke into the already polluted air. Amelia had heard of all of this from Baubo, but had never heard it called America, had never seen for herself the masses and masses of people involved.

Amelia wondered, "How did it end up as Elysium and Freeland?"

Whit pointed at an exhibit. A group of mannequins were arranged to portray a scene. Several people were beating a man, who had collapsed. "Fear. By 2009, the young heterosexuals were dying in record numbers. And that's when the terror began. There was some dementia caused by the disease, but most of the lunacy that occurred was...deliberate and efficient.

"In the East, the states gave up personal freedoms and voted harsh laws into effect, trying to control the spread of the disease. And constitutional rights were gradually eroded until they became non-existent. Instead of trying to cure AGH, people blamed the victims. Supposedly, much of this behavior had started during the early part of the AIDS epidemic and just got worse when it became AGH.

"Then in June, 2010, a select group of white men, the Aryan Procurators, joined forces with a group of religious zealots called the New Order Christians. They convinced the President of the U.S. that something radical had to be done. He issued the Laws of Public Safety. It was supposed to be a temporary measure, but it ended up superseding the U.S. Constitution. Liberty and individual freedoms gave way more and more to regulations, and finally democracy was crushed by Fundamentalist interpretations of the Bible. Not surprisingly, the Aryans and the New Order Christians ended up with all the power. They called the new nation Elysium—which, ironically enough, is Greek for paradise."

Amelia stared at the figure the mannequins were attacking. "They killed the carriers."

"Yes. And anyone else who wasn't white, heterosexual and an avowed Fundamentalist Christian. A tide of refugees came racing west. The states in the middle of the continent, already swamped with their own public health emergency, were just overrun. By 2011, people were dying so fast that the highways were clogged with abandoned cars, nothing but corpses at the wheel. Orphaned children were running in small herds, raiding the supermarkets for canned food, and even eating rodents when packaged food was not to be found. Eventually these children began resorting to cannibalism."

"That's why you didn't want to go near the roads during our trek," Amelia commented.

Whit swallowed. "The towns are even worse. Empty, dilapidated buildings and skeletons all over the place."

They shared the mournful silence for a moment.

"Anyway, most of the west rebelled against the Laws of Public Safety," Whit said, resuming her story. "They sent a cable to Washington D.C., stating that they were a 'free land.' A civil war erupted, what we now call the Great Schism. In 2013, the New Order Christians bombed Las Vegas, the heart of the western resistance. Of course, the radiation made the AGH virus even worse...."

The two women moved before a huge world map. Red dots spread over each continent, showing the far-flung nature of the contagion. Whit continued, "AGH went on to ravage the world. Over one third of the global population was gone by 2017; by 2030, the United Nations, or what was left of it, reported over one half of the world population was dead and many more were dying. In the most hard hit areas—Russia, India, Brazil, China,and much of Africa—the plague meant annihilation. Now, of course, international contact between countries has been reduced to a tribal affair. Today, we have no idea how many people are left globally."

"What about the Border?" Amelia asked. "How did the Elysians ever manage that? I would think it was beyond them."

Whit laughed humorlessly. "In the beginning, they had some of the best minds available. The military-industrial complex, they used to call it. A group of scientists created an invisible photo-electromagnetic shield—an oval of light beams controlled by satellites in space. The Border rose out of the Atlantic Ocean and fell across the center of the continent. It sealed Elysium into its own world, so that no one came in and no one went out. After they killed every Plague-Bearer they could find, they thought they were safe."

Whit contemplated the world map, the red that showed even in Elysium. "Of course, they were wrong. By the time they understood that, they had come to realize the importance of having a population, even a sick one. There were jobs to be done and no one to do them. AGH-free women were turned into Breeders and kept in penitentiaries because there were no longer enough healthy citizens to assure a future Elysian civilization. Now, they post AGH victims on farms in the rural areas, far away from 'normal' people. They slave away their remaining years as serfs, providing food for their rulers. But you know all about that, don't you?"

They regarded each other for another long moment.

Whit cleared her throat. "Meanwhile, in Freeland, only one group of people had survived in vast numbers. These were the ones who didn't have sex with men."

"Lesbians," Amelia stated triumphantly, as if it were all beginning to make sense.

They wandered to the next exhibit. Here was a scene depicting a group of women repairing a corn harvester, surrounded by children.

"When the plague first started, some women in the Pacific Northwest had the foresight to organize. They set up sperm banks and hidden communes. In fact, lesbians seemed to universally disappear during the Great Schism. Then, after the Border went up in 2013, the lesbians began asserting their presence. Secret armies of women warriors came out of the mountains, gathering up survivors. New settlements were built, new life created. Civilization survived. Patriarchy, however, was gone for good."

"Patriarchy?" Amelia asked.

"What you lived with in Elysium—you know—men always being right and in power, just by virtue of the fact that they're men."

Amelia immediately understood.

"Fierce women kept civilization alive," Whit went on. "Now we call them 'the Mothers,' because they brought the next generations into the world. They led their villages, developed inventive methods of food production, expanded medical resources, organized schools. Women worked hard, had large families, and passed on the concept of woman-strength to their daughters and sons.

"Some sperm banks had no categorical descriptions attached to the sample. A woman bore a child and it was considered good fortune, the gift of a future. Racial hybrids were the norm.

"Other women chose to preserve their ethnicity. They searched the banks until they were able to match the donor sample with their own heritage. Since the Elysians were promoting Aryan purity, it seemed essential to some that the Unwanteds be cultivated, too. Japanese, Navaho, African, Vietnamese, Arab, Mexican—the differences were prized and preserved.

"Since the inception of parthenogenesis, most everyone except the heteros have procreated that way. The egg-egg, or double X chromosome children, are preferred to egg-sperm children, who run the risk of having an XY chromosome. Less volatile, they say. I think it's just another form of prejudice, myself."

Amelia asked, "Are you egg-sperm?"

Caught being defensive, Whit nodded, then grinned.

Amelia studied her a moment. "You're not volatile, just...spirited."

Deep brown eyes held her there. The admiration was so direct, so honest, that it made Whit blush.

They both looked down at the floor, each aware that a boundary had been crossed. Amelia finally moved to the large map of Freeland that hung on the wall.

Back turned, Amelia asked, "What happens to the egg-sperm boy babies?"

Whit took the opportunity to regain her composure. "Some mothers make gifts of the boys to the men down in Harvey who wish to raise children, or to the sterile hetero couples in other colonies. Some mothers keep the boys and move to colonies that tolerate the presence of men. You see, men are not allowed in Artemis."

Turning to look at Whit, Amelia questioned, "Why?"

Whit shrugged. "The Mothers wrote the No Males Law into the Articles of Artemis. After all, men have been outlawing lesbians for centuries, and practicing misogyny for thousands of years. It was the intention of the Mothers to have lesbians control not only this colony, but also their lives even after the AGH plague subsided. It is safer for us this way."

"An Amazon nation," Amelia said softly.

"Not quite." Whit went on, "Artemis is one of the seven interdependent colonies. In each one, personal freedoms are guaranteed and individuality is encouraged. We are still governed by the best parts of the old U.S. Constitution. We have a Senate and a House of Representatives. No President, though. That's what got us into trouble the last time. It had gotten to be too much power to leave with one person. Instead of a President, we elect Leaders, like Lilith, in each colony. The seven Leaders have weekly and sometimes daily televisual conferences, and decide issues with majority votes."

Amelia suddenly gave an enormous yawn.

"Am I that bad?" Whit laughed.

"No, no. I'm...so tired I could fall asleep on the floor." A sheepish grin followed the remark.

And for the second time that day, Whit felt something shift within her. Something that had been brittle and stiff, melted.

Whit led the way outside.

*****

Lilith touched the DNA plate and entered the computer files. The section entitled "Isis," appeared on screen. Lilith began reading the history of the mountain colony, from its construction and settlement to its violent end. She shivered as she read about the small garrison of warriors who had battled against hundreds of Regs. Before forces from the other colonies could arrive, granaries had been looted, captured warriors had been burned alive. An entire population had been reduced to ash. Then the Regs had fled safely back to the other side of the Border. And the stench of betrayal had clung to one name.

Maat Tyler. Lilith drew a deep breath as she read it, remembering.

Maat was the computer wizard who had written the codex software, turning the old satellites to new use. The Elysians had erected their shield dome, but within a generation they had lost the intellectual resource to control it. For the Elysians, the Border had become a mystery. Then, after years of study, Maat had rediscovered how to coordinate the satellite beams. The electronic design the Elysians had created to keep the rest of the world out, became a cage enclosing them. When Maat had announced news of her codex, the citizens of Freeland had at last felt safe from the Regs.

Maat had even taken the design one step further and developed a means of breaking the light beams at certain points. She called the weak spots "Bordergates." For a while it had been stylish for the more daring of their warriors to go undercover in Elysium and gather information, coming and going via these Bordergates.

Then gradually, Freeland had become convinced of the steady dissolution of whatever threat Elysium might be to them. The civilization was clearly destroying itself, strangled by its caste system, sexist doctrine, scientific ignorance, religious fanaticism, and the brutality of the Regulators. The AGH that had provoked it all had survived and was still with them, quietly evading their attempts at quarantine.

Maat had become an influential woman in Artemis. She had stated in her proud, august way, that the Elysians were human beings and suffering demanded action. In her opinion, it was time they shared the AGH therapy with Elysium.

Lilith continued reading how, in the early days after the Great Schism, a Seattle doctor, Dr. Kea, had set up an intensive research team. In one series of experiments, she had consulted with Native American healers to obtain an herbal mixture that had immunostimulatory properties. While the active agents remained unknown, the extract had been used for years in the treatment of various infections, and was known to enhance T-cell activity. The research team found that a vaccine derived from dead AGH virus particles, when used in conjunction with the herbal immunostimulator, had a profound protective effect on bone marrow and resulted ultimately in elimination of the virus from the infected patient. After the doctor had died, a plague victim herself, her research assistant, Dr. Satrina, eventually perfected the treatment.

Once the three necessary medicine-plants involved in producing the immunostimulator were successfully introduced to a farming and harvesting regimen, only the actual production of the mixture became a problem. The laboratory preparation was time-consuming and needed a team of botanists and analytical chemists to attain the desired results.

As a young woman, Maat had worked in the lab. It was she who had created the computer program that made the preparation of the immunostimulator a simple automated process. If caught early enough, before multiple organ damage occurred, AGH was defeated by the treatment. And so it was that, within a decade of Maat's contribution, AGH had ceased to exist in Freeland.

Maat's proposal to share the cure with Elysium had been a controversial one. Some women had seen her as a fool, about to endanger all of Freeland. Medical knowledge had become tenuous in the near illiteracy of Elysium, as had the capability to monitor even a simple, computer-run manufacturing program. Others had been convinced that the Elysians would somehow turn the medical technology into a weapon, and then use it against them. And once the Elysians realized Freelanders could open the Bordergates, some had been sure the Elysians would create an opportunity to sneak in and attack. However, many others had seen Maat as a mythical wisewoman—compassionate, all-knowing, able to heal the nation and bring America back.

Maat's amazing intellect and strength had given her station among the women of Artemis. However, it was her insistence that they help Elysium that made her the overwhelming favorite to lead the new colony of Isis.

Lilith had lost her. Maat had been swept up in flattery and power. Lilith, the dashing young pilot who jockeyed the big grain transport ships between the colonies, had been left behind. After twelve years of family life, Maat had grown bored. She had begun spending all her time away from their home. Finally, Maat announced she wanted out of the marriage. She had left for Isis, and had taken her child with her.

Lilith had stayed in Artemis, burying her heartache in work and more work. She had moved from the flight cabin to the granaries office. The decisions grew more complex. In five years,

Lilith had risen to power, too, valued as a planner and a thinker, a wisewoman.

And then Isis had fallen.

Two Elysian troop ships and four fighter heli-jets had done the unimaginable: flown through the northern Bordergate. The gate opening had been gauged wide, allowing the huge, antiquated troop transports to navigate through the screen opening. And the gate had been automatically suspended in the open phase for an eight hour period. It had given the Regs plenty of time to fly to Isis, plenty of time to rape, pillage, burn and then return to Elysium.

In order for the Bordergate to function, someone in Freeland had to trigger the DNA plate. The last DNA code registered in the northern gate had belonged to Maat Tyler. During the grisly days of identifying the dead, they had found Maat among the ash-corpses in the meadow. After weeks of burials, every citizen of Isis had been identified and accounted for, except one.

Though many claimed this citizen's body had been lost, probably disposed of in the fir forest surrounding Isis, many others were suspicious. The lost citizen had been listed as a deserter.

Amelia Earhart, indeed. Only Baubo would come up with such a prankish clue.

How had an enemy army gotten into Freeland? There had never been a definitive answer. Many, Zoe included, believed that Maat had attempted some sort of barter with the Regs. Others, like Lilith herself, still defended Maat. It remained a heated controversy. There were venomous arguments whenever the subject came up, and most of the households in Artemis had learned to avoid the subject in order to keep the domestic peace.

Lilith leaned back, aching as if it had all happened yesterday, not ten years ago.

In Freeland, the records of a citizen's DNA code were preserved, even after death. The codes allowed people to know their family, their history. So the population of Isis lived on in the core computer of their Cedar House. The building had become a memorial, a place where grieving visitors came to call back images and voices and beloved personalities. Nestled high up in the Cascade range, near Mount Tahoma, the grass grew in the streets of Isis and the residents survived in the expanded laser molecular memory of their super computer.

Lilith knew the answer was there.

— 8 —

Two days later, Lilith watched Cimbri cross the tarmac. Even in the scant dawn light, it was obvious that she was moving with a deliberate provocativeness. Lilith looked over at the blonde leaning against the hull of the small ship. She was rummaging through the backpack Lilith had prepared, more intrigued with what they were having for lunch than with Cimbri's show.

Lilith adjusted her gray warrior's tunic. She had gained weight since she had last worn it, that was how infrequent her activities away from a desk had become. Every mouthful she ate seemed to take up permanent residence around her middle.

Amelia, on the other hand, didn't appear to be gaining a pound, despite her seeming obsession with food. Actually, it wasn't that the young woman ate that *much*, it was just that she always seemed to be squirreling away something to eat.

Another figure came running across the landing zone. Amelia glanced in that direction and the apple heading toward her mouth was forgotten. The intent brown eyes stayed on the runner until she slowed to a stop in front of her.

Cimbri joined them and also noticed the way Amelia gazed at Whit. "You're late, Major," she griped.

Whit smoothed her own gray tunic and gave Cimbri an incredulous look. "I arrived before *you*." Seeing Amelia's smile, Whit flashed one back, then swung up the metal stairway and bounded into the jet.

Cimbri followed, the long, white dress she was wearing flouncing. *A white dress on a hike?* Lilith thought. *Cimbri must have a seduction planned.*

Shoving her apple into a deep trouser pocket, Amelia shouldered the knapsack. Lilith noted how well worn and comfortable the dark trousers appeared. And the big, kelly green pullover was familiar. *She's still wearing Whit's clothes.* Lilith suddenly remembered how she herself had once obtained a wondrous comfort from wearing Maat's clothes. Unsettled by the surge of feeling that accompanied the thought, Lilith began the climb up the steep entrance ramp.

Once inside, Lilith resumed command, asking Whit to pilot and then inviting Amelia to sit beside her near the window. She instructed Whit to take the craft up slowly and hug the shore of the Sound before taking the usual flight path.

Noting Amelia's puzzled expression, Lilith laughed softly, knowing yet another question was being hatched. Sure enough, Amelia leaned closer and whispered, "Whit knows computers, farming, and she can fly jets, too? How old is she?"

Amused, Lilith whispered back, "She's thirty, but age has nothing to do with it. Whit has a passion for learning, for mastering new abilities."

Overhearing them, Cimbri turned and murmured, "She's a Renaissance woman." And then Cimbri fixed Whit with a gaze that would have melted a glacier.

Executing the take-off in vertical-mode, Whit was oblivious to all this covert attention. She gradually shifted the power to the jet engines and the aircraft glided forward. Underneath the craft, the city receded, the fishing nets hanging to dry on the Puget Sound beach slid from sight.

Blue water and fir forests swept below them, a visual symphony. Amelia pressed her forehead against the glass, wide-eyed, saying nothing. Cimbri began helpfully pointing out various landmarks and Lilith motioned her silent with a covert gesture.

The craft swung inland, over the patchwork quilt of autumnal crops. Whit dipped the transport lower, until they skimmed the golden grain fields and had to bank in rhythmic swoops to crest the occasional stands of Douglas Firs. The Cascades rose before them, snowy peaks glistening pink in the first touch of October sunlight.

And then Amelia saw the mountain. Lilith heard the quick intake of breath, saw the fists clench. The huge white mound of Mount Tahoma sat poised on the land like a single, elegant breast, beckoning them to come nourish themselves.

Turning pale, Amelia moved back from the window and bent over, hugging her arms across her stomach.

"All this zooming," Cimbri soothed. She reached over to Whit and tapped her. "Calm down, Show-off. You're making her air-sick."

Whit glanced back at Amelia, concerned, then began piloting the craft more conservatively. After several deep breaths, Amelia sat up and the composed mask dropped back in place.

At last, the tarmac appeared below them, the amazingly unblemished landing zone of the community that had once thrived in these mountain meadows. Whit switched on the retro-jets. They landed gently and disembarked.

Cimbri linked her arm through Whit's, murmuring the latest gossip and setting off down the gravel road. Whit gave Amelia an apologetic look, then allowed Cimbri to pull her away.

"Do you know where we are, Amelia?" Lilith asked probingly, as she waded into the tall grass by the landing strip. She watched Amelia look around, eyes crinkling against the sunshine. While Lilith gathered wildflowers, Amelia studied the huge mountain taking up much of the horizon beyond the trees.

Amelia brushed a hand under her eyes and sat down on an out-cropping of rock.

Lilith went over and sat beside her.

Amelia began crying softly. "I feel so awful, yet so good—what's the matter with me?"

Lilith pulled her close and rocked her. "Tell me."

Amelia was sobbing hard. "I want...to run. I want to...stay, to find...."

Lilith brushed a hand over the gleaming hair. "Find what?"

"I can't remember!" Amelia raged, slamming the granite. Lilith caught the scraped hand before the woman brought it down a second time. "Why can't I remember?!" she wailed.

Amelia suddenly leapt up and began running. Lilith watched her racing down the road, knowing where it would lead her.

*****

Cimbri tugged on Whit's arm and steered them down a side street—or what was left of a side street. The firestorm that had swept through Isis had left mostly rubble. A few house shells still stood, blackened hulks of stone that lined the weed-grown roads like silent sentinels of grief.

"We're supposed to meet them at the Cedar House," Whit said, with that wary, vulnerable glance Cimbri treasured.

She stopped, certain Whit would not resist her. She pulled the hard, muscled body against her, caught Whit's head and brought it down, within reach of a searching tongue. Whit shook in her arms, the fierce blast of response pouring helplessly from her, the white-hot desire Cimbri remembered.

Angry, Whit thrust her away. "Stop it!"

Cimbri wanted her so badly then that even this vast graveyard was not going to deter her. She placed her hands on Whit's shoulders and pushed her back against the scorched rock of a napalmed house. Gripping the thick, dark hair, Cimbri brought her lips to just below Whit's and stayed there, waiting. They were so close they were breathing into each other's mouths.

A deep groan came from the back of Whit's throat.

Cimbri undid the gunbelt, lifted the gray warrior's tunic. Whit tried to move away from the wall, but Cimbri pressed into her, capturing a breast in her mouth. For an instant, Whit's body instinctively arched toward her, swelling with passion. Then, all at once, Whit wrestled free. She grabbed up the gunbelt, refastened it around her waist with trembling hands.

Cimbri glared at her. "Don't tell me you don't want it. You want it so badly I can smell it."

Whit picked up the backpack. "I don't want *you*," she said decisively. She left Cimbri cursing behind her.

*****

Amelia walked along, wiping her face on the front of her sweater. Sobs kept climbing out of her, catching on each breath. The stark, fire-blackened mounds of stone showed no definite outline of the buildings they had been. All the same, her mind was flashing with disturbingly vivid images of what those buildings had looked like. It began to be eerie. The great sadness she felt slowly subsided, edged out by a gnawing anxiety.

What's happening to me?

She started running again, following a road, not certain if she was going the right way. She wanted to get back to Lilith, back to the transport ship. She only wanted to leave, now.

She came around a stand of old fir trees and saw a white tower, part of a large wooden building, nestled in a meadow of flowers. She skidded to a stop, recognizing instantly what she had seen in her dreams for years.

The elation she felt stunned her, for she had no concept where it came from, what event, what memory. She only knew that tower, rising above the meadow, brilliant white against an azure sky. Amelia ran to it as if every answer she had ever been denied lay beyond that huge wooden door.

*****

Lilith had taken the shortcut through the deep wood, the walk she had often taken with Maat in the days of young love. She moved slowly, her arthritic knees protesting the struggle over fallen trees and small streams. She made respectful apologies to any spirits she disturbed on this hallowed ground. Drinking in the peace and quietude, she called on Maat to come to her, to help her with this venture.

When she finally emerged from the forest, near the Cedar House, she saw Amelia standing before the large ceremonial door, pulling on the decorative handle.

"That's not the way, my girl," Lilith breathed.

She noticed Whit striding along the road from the city. There was no way to signal her without Amelia seeing them both. Lilith held her breath.

Amelia had to solve the door-riddle alone, had to face The Burned Ones alone. And she deserved the right to confront the true horror before the rest of Freeland descended upon her. If she was who Lilith thought she was, this would only be the beginning of Amelia's trials.

Amelia stood back from the door, hands gripping her hair in frustration. She looked up at the tower for a long moment.

Whit stopped, watching, unseen by Amelia.

Suddenly, Amelia walked to the left. She peered into a group of granite boulders. She reached between the two largest ones and the door glided open. As if in a trance, the young golden-haired woman walked into the Cedar House.

*****

There was light, but after the bright daylight outside, the room seemed dimly lit. Amelia stood still in what seemed like a hallway. The door thudded shut behind her and she jumped.

She could smell something. Candle wax?

Cautiously, she moved down the corridor and saw the stubs of wicks in flat pools of wax, saw the small altars. There were prayer wheels, some small clay Goddesses. All manner of worship was possible in Freeland. Baubo had told her that once, but she had not believed it until now, when her own eyes saw the proof.

Return to Isis

In Elysium there was only Christianity.

The names here—Tomyris, Cimbri, Lilith, Branwen—these were not Christian names. They were the ancient names of Sarmatian Amazons, of Celtic Goddesses and warriors.

She froze. How did she suddenly, out of nowhere, know so damn much? She hadn't known all that about the names before she'd walked through that door.

Clearly, her mind was no longer her own. Thoughts were coming and going of their own will, making no sense at all. She had a tremendous urge to walk straight ahead, into what was a solid stone wall.

The wall soundlessly slid into a sudden crevice in the rock. A large room lay before her. The scent of cedar came, crisp and clean.

She passed through the portal and knew with a certainty surpassing knowledge that she had done this before. She had done it hundreds of times.

This was the Council Room, where the elected leaders met and debated and governed. The circular, dark wooden table was in itself a symbol of power. The huge emblem mounted on the wall at the far end of the hall was a declaration of strength. A six pointed star and a dolphin in the center.

Just like in the dream.

She moved across the room, focusing on one seat slightly more ornate than the others around the table. She suddenly saw her there, the golden-haired woman, turning to greet her with a smile. She took two steps in a rush, ready to drop into her lap, then realized there was no one there.

Amelia went rigid. She could hear herself breathing fast in the still room. Who was that? The sensations—relief, joy, wonder—all the feelings that vision had unleashed in her—she had never even known she could feel that much. Who *was* that?

All at once she felt she had to get out of this place. She could not bear what she was feeling. Across the room, another wall was sliding open.

*****

Whit got to the door just as it thumped closed, sealing Amelia within the Cedar House. She stared at the wood, astonished, then saw Lilith coming through the meadow, waving at her.

"Did you see it?" Whit called. "She opened the door!"

"It's why we came here, Major."

Whit watched Lilith come closer, noting the stiffness in her walk. Then the implication of what Lilith had said settled in. "At the least she's a Freelander."

Lilith chuckled. "More than that, I think."

"You know who she is?"

"I have made a guess, a rather hopeful one. But I am an old woman who has seen much sorrow. I need hope." Lilith handed Whit a palm computer and motioned Whit to reach into the boulders for her.

Whit connected the palm computer with the quartz panel, gathering the data on the DNA that had triggered the door.

"Where is Cimbri?" Lilith asked.

Whit shrugged her shoulders.

"Nursing hurt feelings, I suppose," Lilith guessed.

Handing the palm computer unit back to Lilith, Whit muttered, "She's in the city ruins, being impossible."

Lilith concentrated on running the DNA identification program. and said, "I was afraid that white dress would be your undoing. It would have been, once." Eyes still on the readout panel, a pleased smile overcame her.

Whit waited expectantly.

Lilith said nothing.

Exasperated, Whit snapped, "Must I wait for the Council to convene over this or will you tell me?"

Lilith said, "The way Amelia looks at you—have you noticed it?"

Whit was temporarily thrown. "A crush. She will find me willful and boring soon enough."

"Perhaps not. You also look at her in a special way, Tomyris."

"Why are we always discussing my love life?" Whit shouted.

"Because you are like a daughter to me and I will see you well loved and happy before I die." Lilith held her eyes after that statement.

Whit swallowed. "You are going to live...."

"I am entering my Crone years," Lilith finished.

A long quiet was broken only by twittering birds deep in the forest. Whit gazed at the woman who had cared for her since her own family had perished in The Fall of Isis. The keen blue eyes pierced her, strong and vigilant as ever.

"The woman in that building is going to need our help, Whit. She is going to end up facing Zoe, facing all those in Freeland who mutter that freedom for some is too great a security risk. Each colony has its minorities, each citizen has some tradition to cling to, allowing no compromise. It is only a matter of time until our fear of differences makes us into Elysians. Fear and prejudice are the darker side of human nature."

Whit frowned, not sure she was following. "But Zoe wouldn't bother her if we could prove Amelia was a prisoner of war."

Lilith, taking a deep breath, stated simply, "Her name is Kali, daughter of Maat."

Whit stepped back, shocked.

Then Lilith whispered, "Suspected traitor in the Fall of Isis."

— 9 —

Amelia walked into the next room, perplexed. This chamber was not like the rest of the building. The familiarity no longer throbbed at the back of her skull, making her head ache with the effort to grasp what would not be grasped.

Various machines were clustered neatly together along the wall. She examined the small, shiny surfaces near them. They were like the plates she'd seen Lilith use to work the machines in the Leader's House.

Amelia herself had never been able to make the machines go. Lilith said it was because each person had a unique genetic code and that her code was not registered in the citizens' data bank. If she was granted clearance, they would make her a citizen of Artemis and register her DNA. Until then, she was dependent on others to unlock doors, power the cooking units, and operate any of the other non-classified technology that made life easy in Artemis.

She had grown used to wistfully touching the quartz plates. Out of habit, she reached out.

Her fingers barely made contact. The space before her lit up and other women were in the room with her. Amelia jumped back. *Where did they come from?*

They didn't seem to see her, looked right past her. She stepped forward and her arm caught some of the many beams of light from the walls and ceiling. The transparent images went on with their activities, not noticing her, while part of the scenery glowed on her sleeve.

Hologram, she thought, and right behind the meaning came the surprise of knowing the word.

Women were celebrating some event. An anniversary. Two women were kissing and the crowd around them was applauding. The two women separated, laughing. Amelia suddenly realized it was Branwen, much younger looking, in the arms of the golden-haired woman.

Then, abruptly the scenes changed. Women were walking along the streets of a busy city. One by one, women proudly displayed their homes, their skillcrafts, their schools. The women invited her to join them in building Freeland's newest, most dynamic colony. Then inexplicably, their beams of light shut off, the images vanished.

Amelia blinked. What had she seen?

She noticed a door nearby. Then her eyes were pulled to something very odd.

A large, stone statue of twisted shapes stood a short distance away. Amelia walked closer to it, staring hard at the abstract design. The faces were contorted with pain, the mouths open in silent screams. What was the rippling effect climbing up the legs? Then she saw the shackles on wrists and feet.

A slice of memory tore unexpectedly into that moment. She was in a meadow, in bright sunlight. The women in chains were screaming behind waves of shimmering flame.

Amelia spun away from the statue, doubled over, fell to the polished wooden floor. She lay there gasping until an odd numbness seemed to gather around her. A cottony wall swallowed the whisper of things forgotten.

She lay there for a long while, drifting, unable to focus a thought. Far off, she heard someone calling. She lifted her head. The golden-haired woman leaned against a large, wooden cabinet.

Slender white and black teeth lined the front panels, rows of small buttons covered the top.

Slowly, she got up. The woman beckoned her closer. Amelia stumbled a few steps. Who was this radiant being she knew so well and yet not at all? She came close enough to touch her and stopped, scarcely breathing. The woman motioned toward the keys. Amelia's hand seemed to move on its own remembrance. Bells sounded softly above her. Amelia looked up and saw the inside of the tower, rising overhead. Silver bells were swinging, glancing in sunlight.

She looked back at the woman. No one was there.

*****

Cimbri paced impatiently in front of the Cedar House. "She's been in there too long."

Lilith sat in the grass, braiding the stems of wildflowers. Whit took a long drink from the wine bag and Lilith rebuked her gently, saying, "You're our pilot, you know."

"I've only had a little," Whit returned, then flopped on her back.

Cimbri said, "Gaea! One gets drunk and the other makes daisy-chains! Am I the only adult on this mission?"

Lilith replied, "You are the medical resource. If we wanted over-reaction and ridicule we would have brought Zoe."

Whit giggled.

Cimbri whirled. "Amelia has been in there alone for hours! Don't you care about her?"

Lilith remarked, "An interesting question."

Whit kept silent.

From above them, the soft, warm sound of bells came in four tentative tones. They all looked up at the tower.

Shortly afterward, Amelia opened the door and ran to them. Cimbri caught the young woman's chin in her hand, noting the tear-reddened eyes.

Amelia gently broke the grip. "I'm alright."

Cimbri guided her to the grass. She emptied her medical pouch on the overgrown lawn, searching for the somascanometer, and insisted on assessing her vital signs. Lilith reached for Amelia, pulling the blonde head to her lap. Amelia stretched out wearily. While Cimbri ran her tests, Lilith caressed the smooth cheek. With her eyes closed, Amelia said, "I can't talk about it just yet. Is that okay?"

"That's okay," Lilith replied soothingly.

"It's coming to me in crumbs, like never enough for supper in Elysium. And I'm so hungry." Amelia sighed.

"It will come," Lilith soothed, stroking her brow.

"No, I mean really hungry. Where's that pack?"

Lilith laughed. Amelia sat up and found Whit spreading cheese, fruit and bread on a cloth.

*****

Lilith watched the three young women. They ate quietly, the air full of unasked questions and unresolved possibilities. Cimbri gave Whit sulky glances. Whit carefully ignored her and nursed the wine bag. The gray eyes kept straying to Amelia. Amelia sat hunched over, her face flickering with one half-formed emotion after another. Lilith noticed the squint.

"Your head aches, Amelia?"

A hand slunk up to her temple. "A little."

Cimbri went to her, pressed her fingers tentatively into Amelia's neck. Then Cimbri noticed Whit's attention. She began massaging Amelia's shoulders. Amelia sat stiffly, tensing against the touch.

Lilith reached into Cimbri's discarded medical pouch and palmed a small container. A few minutes later she asked, "Don't you have any powder, Cimbri?"

Cimbri left Amelia and searched the pouch, very surprised to discover she had no salicylic.

Lilith said, with great resignation, "Let Whit take over."

Cimbri looked disconcerted.

Whit dropped the wine bag.

"Cimbri, come with me and help me find some meadowsweet," Lilith commanded. "Whit will need it later, too, with all the wine she's drunk."

Cimbri peered at Lilith before reluctantly following her.

They crossed the meadow and headed into the deep wood. The stream where the herb grew was not very far, but Lilith decided she would have to take many rests on this gathering expedition. She couldn't help wondering how much of young Kali remained in the woman Amelia.

*****

"Are you good at curing headaches?" Amelia asked.

Whit blushed. In Artemis, that remark was a droll invitation to lovemaking. Did Amelia know what she had just requested? The blonde head bent lower. Amelia covered her eyes with a hand and Whit's uncertainty vanished.

She moved behind Amelia and sat in the tall grass, rubbing the knots in the slender slope of neck and shoulders. The sun baked down. Yellow hair shifted in the languid, autumn breeze, brushing over Whit's hands as she worked. The tension beneath her fingers gradually eased, the muscles in Amelia's back went liquid. Bees hummed in fragrant flowers all around them. The wine began to assert itself in a swirl of arousal. Whit's touch became stronger, surer.

This was Kali, Maat's child. This was the young girl Whit had last seen at the Pledge Ceremony, standing shyly before the crowd in her new warrior's clothing. Maat had been so proud, so annoyed. Maat's ambition for the girl had been thwarted and everyone there had known it. Kali had been groomed to be a scientist. But at twelve the girl had openly rebelled, had quit Maat's laboratory and enlisted as a warrior. At fourteen she had donned her first uniform and taken a posting right here in Isis. Maat had been furious.

Whit herself had watched the coltish adolescent with interest. Kali had been five years younger than she, out of bounds due to their unequal ranks and her youth. But even then, the rumors about her had been flying. The other officers said she was like her mother, clever but headstrong.

Whit couldn't remember the exact details, but there had been some scandal, she was sure of it. Something about sneaking off base to be with a secret lover. Maat had given her the maximum penalty—all the most demeaning, mundane duties. They had said that Maat was trying to break her and Kali knew it. The girl had been posted as guard at the Cedar House, where the codex was kept, for months, right up until the day Isis fell.

Amelia stirred beneath her hands, turned around. Whit looked into pensive brown eyes. *Does she even know her true name?* Whit opened her mouth, determined to ask. Soft, questioning lips swallowed the words.

The sweetness of that kiss led to several others, a series never quite ending or beginning. Logic told Whit to stop. Things were already complicated enough. *But, oh Goddess, I want her.* She found herself pulling Amelia down in the grass.

The kisses quickly became feverish. Whit slid her hands up under the kelly green sweater, feeling with her fingertips the planes of that long coveted back. Amelia rolled on top of Whit, her hands in Whit's hair, kissing and trembling and slowly, but most definitely, taking command.

Whit felt herself losing control, so lost in sensations that she couldn't think or resist. Her own voice was betraying her, mewing like a small cat each time Amelia circled a palm across her breasts. She was reacting helplessly, writhing with desire. Somehow, her gun belt was gone, and then her tunic was opened and pulled off. Grass tickled, poked her back, further inciting the passion unleashed by the hands moving over her.

Her trousers were opened, tugged from her hips. Amelia's hands lightly smoothed the insides of Whit's thighs, magically making them open wider, wider. The fingers barely touched her, passing almost reverently over her until Whit was lurching after them. She was frenzied, consumed with the need for completion.

"Do you know what to do?" Whit gasped.

Amelia pulled her sideways. All of Whit's body weight leaned into the fingers gliding in and out of her. Whit lost whatever control she had left. She was spinning, falling through the blue sky above them. And Amelia took her, as expertly as Cimbri had ever done, as thoroughly, as relentlessly. Whit's entire being was exploding, gathering again, exploding. She could only cling to the woman and sob with the joy of it.

After what seemed like a long time, she found herself sighing, falling onto her back, gazing up into blue. Amelia lay beside her, the honest brown eyes full of passion, hiding nothing.

Whit rose up on an elbow, reached for her.

Amelia pushed her back. "I can hear Lilith whistling."

Whit cocked her head and the faint tune registered. Amelia helped her into her clothes. They brushed grass seed off each other, the strokes growing more intimate, becoming caresses. At last Whit gave up the attempt for appearances and pulled the woman down again.

Whit breathed, "Have you ever...?"

"I don't think so," Amelia whispered back.

Whit moved closer to her. "I want you like that."

Amelia started trembling.

Whit kissed her, softly persuading with her lips and tongue.

Amelia surrendered. Brown eyes dark with lust, she allowed herself to be positioned. She was riding Whit's leg before Lilith and Cimbri even cleared the wood. Whit gripped the straining buttocks, holding Amelia's yoni tight against her thigh. Even through the clothes, it so obviously felt good to her. Whit employed a finger, tickling between the leg, and hot crotch. Amelia flung her head back. The lusty, guttural cry split the mid-afternoon hush, echoing across the meadow. Whit couldn't help laughing as Amelia slouched and then rolled off her.

There could be no pretense now. Somehow, it was both a delight and a relief. Whit gazed at the woman breathing hard next to her, hoping this was not a mere satisfaction of desire. The brown eyes held her, acknowledged the bond between them. Was this to be her partner, then—this woman she had found in an Elysian ditch?

The grass nearby snapped with footsteps and they looked up into two very different faces. Lilith seemed shrewdly satisfied. Cimbri glared at them.

"Meadowsweet, indeed," Cimbri grumbled. She spun on a heel and headed back toward the ship.

"I think we all are ready to go home," Lilith said. She watched the women rise from their flattened-out spot, grass stems every which way in their hair and clothes. She added, "Whit, you may as well get your gear out of the barracks and move into your old room."

"Your old room?" Amelia asked, puzzled.

Whit explained, "I was studying crop management in Artemis. My family was...here. Lilith took me in, became my second family. I, like many others, had such sorrow...I sort of lost my way for a while."

Amelia nodded. She plucked grass stems with extreme care, then finally ventured, "Was I here when the city fell?"

Whit and Lilith exchanged looks. Whit answered, "Yes."

Amelia faced the quiet, early October field. "Am I the only one left alive?"

"Yes."

Amelia stood studying the exquisite beauty and peace of the scene. No one spoke.

She moved away, the shoulders slumped with a sudden emotional weight. They fell in step behind her, wading through the high grass back to the road.

Urgency in her voice, Lilith whispered to Whit, "Zoe has demanded Council for the day after tomorrow. We have medical proof, now, that Amelia is a born Freelander. Granting or withholding clearance is no longer the issue.

"Once Zoe learns who she is, things are going to move fast. The charges against Maat have never been laid to rest. Amelia will be accused of being an accomplice to treachery. Her very survival will be cited as proof of her guilt."

Whit readjusted her pack, the glory of the day suddenly gone with Lilith's truth. She watched Amelia walking before them, head down, no doubt struggling against the limits of memory. Whit's heart ached for her, and she was filled with foreboding.

— 10 —

During the short flight back to Artemis, Lilith began outlining their strategy. They would request a postponement, hoping that in the next few weeks Amelia could remember more about her past. Cimbri cautioned Lilith that Amelia's psyche could not be rushed, that perhaps they were already going too fast. Whit speculated that the amnesia might be permanent. Cimbri jabbed her with an elbow and shot a glance in Amelia's direction.

Why are they protecting me? Amelia wondered. *They hardly know me.*

She listened to them talking, but it was Lilith who held her attention. The keen blue eyes flitted back and forth, monitoring the instrument panel and the luminous western horizon as she talked. She piloted the small jetcraft with an ease that betrayed the work she had done before taking the helm as colony Leader.

Lilith landed the craft with a relaxed competence. While Cimbri and Whit gave suggestions about handling various Council personalities, Amelia studied the older woman. That inexplicable sense of familiarity was once more gnawing within her.

It was after sunset when they returned to Artemis. Lilith, Cimbri and Whit set off through the quiet streets at a brisk pace, still discussing how to bring about a postponement. Amelia trailed behind them, dazed with fatigue. She wanted to ask Whit to sleep with her, to stroke her hair, but she was afraid Whit would run from being so openly needed.

How do I know that? she wondered. *How do I know that some women run from being needed?*

Lilith came back, put an arm about her shoulders. "You look tired. I think it's time you went to bed..."

Amelia didn't hear another word. She saw a younger woman, dark-haired, blue eyes shining. The woman was bending down, handing her a ragged, stuffed doggie, telling her that it was time for bed. Images began tumbling by her: a woman piloting a jetcraft, making her squeal with each swoop and dive; a woman dancing across a grassy lawn, teaching her the warriors' style of kick-fighting; a woman pulling covers over her, kissing her good night.

"Lil," Amelia asserted. "You're my Lil." The words caught in her throat.

A long, frozen moment. Then at last, Lilith nodded.

The earth tilted sideways. Lilith's arms wound round her.

*****

The next morning, Whit hurried into the clinic. Cimbri looked up from the youngster she was treating, frowned, and asked what she wanted. Whit said she'd wait in the office.

Impatiently, Whit rolled up the sleeves of her faded, denim workshirt, annoyed now that she had dressed so quickly. If she was going to see Amelia, she wanted to look better than this.

Moments later, the little girl trotted in to show Whit her brand new cast. As the child left, Cimbri appeared in the doorway, saying, "That one will be you in another twenty years. She just won a dare. Broke her arm, mind you, but won the dare."

Whit grinned. "Good for her."

Cimbri came closer and Whit moved away.

"Are you here on business or pleasure?" Cimbri inquired, a suggestive smile on her face.

"Business. Get your med-kit."

Cimbri took a sideways step and Whit realized she was being maneuvered into a corner.

"Cimbri, this is important."

Cimbri moved in, kissed her.

Whit didn't respond. She simply waited for her to stop. Cimbri cursed, tossed her gleaming black braids, pushed Whit away.

Whit continued, "It's Amelia. Lilith just called. She asked me to bring you."

Cimbri folded her arms, clearly jealous.

"After Lilith sent us away last night, she thought Amelia went to bed. Instead, she's been up all night, pacing around her room, trying to make herself remember more. She seems to have trouble talking and keeps lapsing into...staring spells."

Cimbri fastened her pouch around her waist. "I told Lilith we were going too fast. Damn it!"

Whit had been concerned, but not alarmed. The alarm set in with Cimbri's reaction, with the way Cimbri ran down the street.

*****

They found Lilith in the corner of Amelia's room, holding Amelia, rocking her. Cimbri knelt beside them. Amelia was staring into empty space.

While Cimbri did a preliminary physical exam, Whit stood aside feeling clumsy and useless. Cimbri tried to break through to Amelia in a variety of ways, then called Whit over.

"You're her lover, right?" Cimbri asked.

Whit equivocated, "Well, I hope so, but it was only that once, yesterday..."

Impatient, Cimbri rushed on, "If anyone can penetrate this defense, it's you. She's going catatonic. Touch her. Make her react to you. She may allow you in, even to that place where no one else may enter."

Cimbri took the tense fist from Amelia's lap and handed it to Whit. She signalled Lilith. They rose and left the room.

Whit sat holding the clenched hand, looking into unseeing brown eyes. She spent several minutes calling her name, then fell silent.

How can I reach her? How can I pull her back from the edge?

Amelia removed her fist, pressing it against her temple. *Her head hurts*, Whit thought.

Whit glanced at the bed nearby. She stood and grasped Amelia. She carried her to the bed, laid her on it. Now she was on familiar ground. She knew what to do about a headache.

Whit slowly opened the buttons of Amelia's red shirt, removing it, and the buff trousers and leather boots. She went to the bath and returned with a small basin of cold water and a soft terry cloth. Dipping the cloth in the bracing water, Whit began by cooling Amelia's forehead, face and neck, but ended with lascivious strokes around her nipples, abdomen, and clitoris. She couldn't help herself. The lithe body began responding, encouraging her.

Whit set the cloth and bowl aside. She stripped off her own clothes, then arranged Amelia on her belly, face turned. She mounted the firm, round buttocks, ran strong hands up Amelia's rigid back. The Reg's sword had left an angry crescent on the right shoulder. Whit leaned over, massaging carefully around fresh, pink scar tissue. She worked her way around the spine, digging her thumbs into the tense chords of muscle.

"I need you." The sound of her own voice made her fully accept what she already knew was truth. "Come back to me...Amelia...Kali...."

Leaning down, Whit kissed her hair, breathed in the fresh scent of her. "I don't care what your name is. I know who you are, and I love you." She whispered in the softness of her upper ear, "Do you hear me, my beautiful friend? I love you."

The whisper made Amelia twitch.

Encouraged, Whit kept running her hands over that fair skin, kept crooning love-talk in a low voice. After a while, Amelia was emitting a soft "Oomph" with each ripple of fingers. Whit brushed the blonde hair aside and began nuzzling Amelia's neck. Her hands slid around and under, cupping breasts, fingering nipples.

"Whit?" The name was almost a moan.

"Right here."

"What happened?"

"Turn over." Whit grasped the hips, helped her flip face up. Amelia looked bleary-eyed, tired. Whit lay full on her, the softness exquisite.

"Sweet Mother, I love you." Whit murmured.

They kissed deeply. Whit tried to end it there, tried to snuggle them both down for a nap. Amelia would have none of it. She whispered, "Whatever you were doing to me, please finish it. I feel a river flowing between my legs." She caught Whit's hand and brought it to the source.

At the mere touch of fingers, Amelia arched. Chuckling, Whit drew her hand away, sent the fingertips gliding over the flat stomach, the small breasts.

"Please," Amelia pleaded. "Now..." She gave a small yip as Whit's fingers found a sensitive area near her elbow.

"Oh, no," Whit answered. "That was the wrong way to break you in, woman. A trousered leg in a meadow—a rush job if ever there was one. No, I'm going to play this marvelous body and make you sing."

As if on cue, Amelia began a low cry that went higher in register as Whit's hands ran the length of her trunk. Whit straddled her, hung her head down and brushed dark hair across taut, pink nipples. She barely kissed Amelia, reared back and smiled at her, delighted that Amelia was so vocal.

Amelia whispered, "I'll make you want it just as badly, then." She rose up and her mouth took possession of a nipple. Whit's head dropped back, her hands coursed up Amelia's back. They fell back on the bed together, both of them singing, now.

So many tones, so many vibrations.

Whit pulled away, slipped down between Amelia's legs. Amelia rose up again, asking, "What are you...?" Whit's tongue made contact with the heat and wetness and the question ended.

Slowly, deftly, Whit gave her the kiss of Artemis, the kiss of lesbians. Gradually increasing and then slackening the pace, Whit sent Amelia into total frenzy; she was rigid one minute, limber the next. Whit eased a finger into the drenched yoni, began a gentle rhythm. Amelia began saying Whit's name over and over, as if adrift on a wild river and calling for help. Amelia clutched Whit's hair, and froze.

Whit knew a strong, gifted tongue could cleave a woman open, could take a woman to physical realms almost unimaginable until the brink was reached and the gate flung wide. Whit also knew a finger stroke on that deep-within place could unleash pure rapture.

What Whit didn't know was how transcendent it would feel to do this to Amelia—to feel, hear, see this particular woman enter nirvana.

The great quiver that shot through Amelia also shot through Whit; the voice that sang had accompaniment. Gazing at Amelia, pink with orgasmic flush, Whit sank against a thigh and realized they had come together.

Very soon, Amelia entreated, "Come here."

Whit moved to her side and held her.

She began shyly, "Whit, is it okay...would you mind if...." There was a long pause, as if Amelia were gathering her nerve. "Would you sleep with me again, like you used to on our journey to Artemis, only with this too, sometimes?"

Whit had said yes four times and kissed her cheek twice before she seemed to realize that Whit was not refusing.

And then, just as Whit was smug with success, Amelia ambushed her. Fingers slipped against her soaking cleft and Whit was suddenly defenseless, accessible. Her legs fell open, her breasts were offered up for tasting, her compliance was immediate and complete.

No one has ever done this to me—triggered me, ruled me with such hungry authority. Then rational thought was gone and her body was simply a kinetic reaction.

Later on, Lilith and Cimbri peeked in and found them beneath the covers, sleeping. The strong aroma of woman-sex disclosed everything. After retreating, Lilith remarked, "If you had been practicing medicine in my day, Cimbri, I'd have been camping on your doorstep."

Cimbri smiled sadly. "It's not just the physical union, though that has its own healing power. Those two have found the essence."

Lilith linked arms with her, said smilingly, "There are cats in town that have many houses. They are happy only when visiting, and belong only to themselves. In the country there are barn cats, who have been alone too long. They want more than visiting; they yearn for a hearth fire and a comforting hand."

Cimbri wiggled her eyebrows. "Well, Dear Sage, can you recommend a house that needs visiting?"

"As a matter of fact, Nakotah called here earlier, looking for someone to share her liberty."

Cimbri stroked her chin. "A likable woman, that Nakotah." She flashed a grin at Lilith and headed down the stairs.

*****

Amelia gazed around the Cedar House, watching the women of Artemis. They clustered together in groups that kept forming and re-forming, the eyes moving as much as the mouths. She noticed that the eyes often lingered on her. She felt uncomfortably alone here in the center chair, enclosed by the circular wooden table.

She gazed at Whit, across the room, doing last minute politics with a group of hard-eyed older women. She saw Cimbri smiling and charming the younger crowd near the door. Nakotah and Griffin smiled to her from their position as sentries.

Amelia gripped the armrests of the chair, her flesh tickling with nerves. No matter what anyone else did for her among these women, she was going to have to make the vital effort on her own behalf. She was going to have to tell the whole tale, even the parts that still lurked behind a veil. Those shadow shapes frightened her most of all.

A big-boned, Mexican woman stared at her from the front row, the black eyes drilling into her mercilessly.

A voice whispered in Amelia's ear. These are your people. Don't be afraid. She turned, anxious to see who was at her side. No one was there.

How could that be?

The Mexican woman stared at her even harder.

Lilith, looking noble and composed as ever, came in and the others all moved to their seats. Lilith sat and they all sat. The authoritative voice called the Council to order. The room fell silent.

In her clear, resonant voice, Lilith read a petition asking for a delay in the clearance considerations. She had barely finished the opening statement when Amelia called out, "Please, if it's alright, I'd rather get it over with." Lilith looked surprised, but put the paper aside and said no more.

Zoe stood up self importantly and walked to the center of the room. She stated that she was submitting a petition against granting clearance to Amelia the Elysian.

Shaking her spiked hair with the vehemence of her words, Zoe launched into a long diatribe against Elysians. She cited the Great Schism, the Bombing of Vegas, the Murder of Unwanteds, the Border—all the bad history that had led to the creation of Freeland. Some eyes were fierce with agreement, some eyes were glassy and bored. Then, her voice hard and icy, Zoe began to talk of Isis, of The Burned, of the possibility that Artemis could fall under Elysian sneak attack. The eyes on Amelia grew narrow with suspicion.

Zoe stopped addressing the crowd and turned to Amelia. "My mother was made a human torch. How do you defend this hideous atrocity, Elysian? Why should we trust anyone from a people that has committed such horrible crimes against humanity?"

Amelia felt the heavy silence drop over her.

Zoe looked eager to continue her monologue.

Amelia said quietly, "I am not an Elysian."

There was a sound like a flock of birds rising. The women all moved, turned to their neighbor, leaned forward to hear.

Amelia said, "I am Kali, daughter of Maat."

Bedlam broke loose. Lilith hammered the gavel, demanding order. Zoe stood slack-jawed for a moment, then lunged for Amelia. The chair went over and they rolled across the floor.

Amelia felt two punches. Instinct took command and she punched back hard. She found herself standing over Zoe, fists up. Zoe lay on the floor holding her ribs.

Someone said, "Mother, you're fast." Whit was beside her. "Give me a chance to save you, next time." But Whit sent a nervous look at the crowd.

Amelia dropped her fists, chagrined. Fighting the well-respected Captain Ference was going to get her nowhere with these women.

Lilith bellowed, "Anyone who plans on seeing the finish of this hearing had better be in her seat and be civilized. The sentries have orders to eject agitators!"

The women returned to their seats. Several friends helped Zoe to her feet. She shook off their support, straightened her gray tunic. She went to her chair and dropped into it angrily, mean green eyes on Amelia.

Amelia glanced at Lilith and got the go-ahead signal. She stood, cleared her throat. The chatter hushed.

She began simply, "I am Kali Tyler. Cimbri the Healer has DNA samples that prove my claim. I have very little memory of my youth. I am used to the name Baubo gave me. Please continue to call me Amelia. As yet, I remember so little of this person Kali...I do not feel I can answer to that name.

"Over the last few days, I have...seen things. They come like waking nightmares. There are still things I cannot bring out of...the mist that shrouds my past. I will try to answer your questions. I am hoping that, with time, I can remember everything."

"How did you live when all the others died?" a voice called, rich with denunciation.

"What happened at Isis?" someone shouted.

"Your mother let the Regs in!" another accused angrily.

A chorus of voices rose, then a deafening roar. Fingers pointed at her, the accusations drowned out in the noise of anger. Lilith repeatedly slammed the gavel, but the crowd only grew louder.

Amelia felt a cold fear grip her chest. She couldn't answer these questions. She still didn't remember the important details.

From the corner of her eye she noticed the golden-haired woman standing behind Lilith. She thought distractedly, that's the woman in the hologram—the woman in the dreams. Then, the black-eyed Mexican woman left her seat, shouting, "Maat! Maat stands with Lilith!"

The shout ended the furor like rain dampening a fire. Women craned their heads, jostling to see the Leader's chair. Amelia heard the echo of the name. "Maat?" The golden-haired woman, her mother, nodded at her.

"Styx, we see nothing," a voice complained.

"I tell you I see her! And so does her daughter!" the Mexican woman answered, approaching Amelia with astonished eyes.

Amelia studied the woman she saw clearly, hovering behind Lilith's shoulder. *This is my mother.* Of course. Why hadn't she known that?

"A ghost? Here? Why?" someone demanded.

Styx answered, "Her daughter knows."

"I do?" Amelia heard herself ask.

And then, her mind unlocked. There were chains on her hands and feet. She was sitting in the sunshine, in a meadow, in a crowd of captured warriors. Green-jacketed Regs passed among them, seizing women, dragging them to the stakes. There was smoke...the smell, the stench...she couldn't breathe.

A harsh male voice was growling, "Where is the key?!"

She was being dragged by the scruff of her tunic, into the smoke. Women were casting terrified eyes at her as the Reg hauled her past. They were all going to burn, they knew it. The Regulators were intent on making this invasion memorable for Freeland.

She was dragged past a woman they were beating. Blood ran from her nose, her front teeth were gone. It was Themis Ference, shrieking, "They can't find the key!" and then laughing with a kind of mad triumph.

Amelia shot a glance at the Cedar House and saw that the huge wooden door was scarred, but still safely intact. Earlier attempts to break down the door had set off the force field; the entire building and the codex hidden within it, were safe behind an impenetrable, invisible shield. In frustration, the Regs were throwing themselves into a hysteria of looting and raping and burning. In the distance, beyond the fir forest, Elysian heli-jets dove low over Isis, dropping napalm. Leaping, orange flames were clearly visible over the tree line. She knew the Regs had come for the codex, the precious computer program that controlled the Border. Once the Elysians had the software and regained the knowledge of how to operate it, Freeland would be exposed. The Border would cease to exist. Every colony in Freeland would be vulnerable to the Reg foraging raids. Every sack of grain, every fish in their clean rivers, every woman—would be taken, taken until Freeland had become a corrupted, festering, dying mass of humanity, like Elysium.

The Regulator shook Amelia, demanding the truth. She felt a brief wave of what-the-hell defiance and let loose a string of curses. The Tribune heard her and came closer, his eyes playing over her as if she were great entertainment. He reached out, fingered her hair.

"Where is the key to the force field, Little One?" the Tribune asked in a deadly sweet voice.

She turned her head quickly and sank her teeth into his thumb.

The Tribune howled, snatched his hand back. Laughing harshly, he said, "Train her, but don't spoil her looks."

The Reg proceeded to beat her until her whole body ached and her ears buzzed like an angry hive. The Tribune finally ordered the Reg away from her.

Slowly, she knew that she was face up on the grass. She knew by the pain that she was alive. The Tribune was stroking her hair, remarking on her age, asking if she, too, was a lesbian. He began a long lecture about the waste of women loving women when men were in need of disease-free Breeders in Elysium.

She was so afraid. She had wet herself during the beating. She was choking on the smoke. She pulled and pulled against the metal shackles, desperate, now. This mild-voiced Tribune frightened her more than the crazed Reg had.

The Tribune hauled her to her feet, grabbed a handful of hair and yanked her head back. Her mother was being chained to the black stake, the gruesome husks of the ones who had gone before still flickering around her.

"Tell me where the key is, Little One," the Tribune said. His voice was silky, his hand stroked her breast.

Themis was chained beside Maat. Maat reached out, gripped her hands, drew Themis close to her. Themis began wailing, another voice among the hundreds echoing across the meadow. Maat looked at Amelia and said, calmly, "You chose to be a warrior. Do your duty. They will kill us, anyway."

"Burn the witch!" the Tribune ordered.

A Reg nearby lifted a rifle barrel. Liquid fire streamed over Themis and Maat. Themis was engulfed entirely and fell. Maat stood, her lower half a flame, the upper half a twisting, screaming pillar.

Amelia felt, saw the white fog surround her. The voice went on screaming.

Gradually, she became aware that hands were gripping her. She could hear a low, husky voice talking. "Come back to me. Come on." The white, swirling fog receded a bit.

Amelia tried to sit up and a brown woman pushed her down again. Many voices were talking, though the tone was muted, like water over mossy rocks.

"Tell me where you are?" the brown-skinned one insisted. For an instant, Amelia drew a blank. Then she saw her. "Whit!" she whispered and landed in those strong arms. The husky voice exhaled, "This hearing is over!"

— 11 —

"No, Whit, we must see this thing through," Lilith commanded. "Everyone sit down, please."

The women shifted back quietly in their seats. Amelia trembled in Whit's sheltering arms. She noticed the woman they called Styx crouching nearby, staring at her, awestruck.

The sound of quiet weeping surrounded them.

Lilith said, "Styx, am I right in assuming we all experienced the same visions?"

Styx nodded. "It was a mind-bond, yes. Her thoughts had such power—I went in and then I couldn't get out—"

"It was a trick!" Zoe cried, her voice strangled.

Styx retorted, impatient, "I gave her a psychic nudge and her memory took us all."

Lilith asked, "Has Amelia suffered any damage?"

Styx came closer, placed a hand on Amelia's head. "The damage is from long ago," Styx replied. "The Regs used many drugs on her. I can sense an odd mixture of chemical residue in the neural tissue."

Zoe hissed, "She gave them the codex!"

Lilith stated flatly, "She gave them nothing. Otherwise, the Regs would have returned, would have raided other colonies."

Impatient, she finished, "The Regs never found the key to the force field! They never got near the codex!"

Zoe placed a booted foot on the table, leapt up on it and exhorted the women of Artemis. "She is alive! All the others burned!" Turning on Amelia, Zoe pointed an accusatory finger. "What did you do to stay out of the fire?!"

Clutching her forehead, Amelia's answer was almost a whimper. "I don't know."

Whit stood up, her face red with suppressed rage. "Leave her alone, Zoe!"

Facing the Council, Styx tried to explain. "What Kali saw in that meadow broke her. The Regs tried to make her remember, to free the information they wanted. The drugs only drove her memories deeper, into her unconscious, where they still exist, in absolute clarity and exactness.

"I think what we saw is the vivid split reality preserved in Kali's brain. For her, ten years ago is now; ten years ago is slipping between the spaces of each present moment and invading her existence."

Amelia realized a plea was being made for her. Was her life on the line, then? In spite of all this pain, was she still contending with the suspicion of these people—her people?

The women of Artemis, sniffling and shocked, were obviously still capable of evaluating her. A roomful of eyes, red-rimmed and watery, bored into her.

Amelia bowed her head, the throbbing pain defeating her, making her death seem an eventuality. They would brand her a traitor and then kill her. Freeland was not so much different from Elysium, after all.

Zoe shouted, "Maat was the traitor and her daughter was her accomplice! Kali deserted the warriors! She became an Elysian! *Death* to this renegade!"

For an instant, an electric tension seemed to crackle across the air. Then, a voice roared, "*Fool!*"

All the eyes in the room riveted on Whit.

"Maat burned alive!" Whit let that hideous reminder sink in before saying anything else. "The Regs forced her daughter to watch!"

A few women broke into helpless sobs. Faces turned toward Amelia again, distraught, compassionate faces. Whit hurled her words at Zoe. "They took Kali into Elysium in chains! She was a *captive!* "

"She should have burned!" Zoe shrieked, her self-control gone, tears streaming down her small, pinched face.

"Look what they did to her!" Whit shouted. She stretched her arm towards Amelia, addressed the Council directly. "They beat her, drugged her, starved her." Her arm dropped, her voice went a pitch lower. "But she was a warrior, trained in slyness, drilled in the art of escape. She got away—Goddess be praised—she got away. She survived."

Women leaned forward, hanging on every word.

"Her memory did not. She came back and knew none of us. And instead of joy at the return of a lost warrior, she comes home to *this!* We accuse her of treachery, of involvement in the worst crime in the herstory of Freeland."

Someone called out, "If she escaped them, why didn't she come back sooner?"

Dark hair lifted, gleaming in the light as Whit turned toward the voice. "Could it be that Baubo knew our real nature? Did she know that, like the Elysians, we'd be more interested in blaming the victim than in helping her?"

Another woman demanded, "Lilith, what was Baubo's mission? None of us has ever known. This is no time for secrets."

Lilith sounded weary, sad. "I gave Baubo no mission. She simply went into Elysium of her own will. I only know what the rest of you know. She sent messages periodically; in one communication she informed us she was training an apprentice."

The Council members sat back or turned to their neighbor, their faces resigned.

From atop the table, Zoe declared, "There are too many holes, Major."

Return to Isis

Whit called to Styx, "When was the last mind-bond?"

Appearing startled, Styx replied, "Eleven years ago, 2082. There was a lost child at Isis and we sought out who had seen her last. We found the direction she had gone, the path she had taken, even found the child before the wet, spring night harmed her."

Whit called, louder this time, "Who served as Bonder?"

Styx laughed. Her eyes snapped with sudden comprehension. "We bonded through Baubo."

The women all leaned forward again.

"Who found the child?" Whit let the question hang there.

An elusive memory surfaced in Amelia's mind. A-five-year-old sitting among the ferns, whimpering, arms stretched out toward her as she came through the fir trees. Amelia spoke up, very softly. "I did. I heard her crying."

"For the record," Whit said clearly, "Kali heard the child crying and joined the search party. Styx, you and I were part of that search party. Did you hear a child crying?"

"No," Styx answered. "None of us heard a child. Kali heard the crying in Isis, over three miles away from where the little girl was eventually discovered."

"And what did Baubo think of that?" Whit asked.

Styx said, "Baubo wanted Kali to study with her. Maat said it was bad enough having a warrior for a daughter, said she wouldn't abide having 'a witch,' too."

A poignant hush filled the hall.

Whit concluded, "Council of Artemis, I give you Baubo's apprentice."

A low, collective noise of agreement came from the group.

Zoe surveyed them all, furious. "Why do you listen to her?! She is under a love spell!" Zoe jumped off the table, advanced ominously on Amelia.

Swiftly, Whit blocked the space between them.

They squared off, and for an instant it looked as if they would fight. Then, Nakotah slammed up the entrance leaf in the circular table, strode across the floor and inserted herself between the two gray uniformed women.

Amelia slowly got to her feet.

Zoe moved away from Nakotah and Whit, green eyes narrowed on Amelia. "You should have died at Isis!" she hissed. "You should have burned, like my mother! Your survival convicts you!" She turned, vaulted across the table and left the hall. Amelia watched her go, wondering if she was right.

*****

Two weeks later, Lilith sat in the Leader's chair, surveying the hall. The circular table had been removed, making way for long banquet tables and a large space for dancing. Platters of fruit, breads and savory vegetable dishes surrounded her. Festive, multi-colored streamers hung from the huge ceiling rafters. Citizens streamed by, arrayed in gay fashions, laughing and bantering. The musicians were tuning up their instruments, a discordant noise above the buzz of the crowd.

She wasn't sure if it was the result of the bountiful harvest or the aftermath of the mind-bond, but this seemed to be the most festive Kern Supper in years.

Readjusting her long jacket, smoothing her loose pants, Lilith cut a glance to her right. She was pretending she couldn't overhear the women nearby who ringed Whit, discussing colony politics. Outfitted in dress uniform, dark hair brushed back from her serious face, Whit looked like some mythic Amazon. The young women were challenging her, demanding solutions for current problems. The older ones were silent, their eyes moving subtly over the tight fitting black pants and wine-red warrior's jacket. The elders had already evaluated Whit and accepted her as a potential Leader. Now they permitted themselves the luxury of just looking at her.

Cimbri swept up in a long, violet dress and lowered herself gracefully into the chair beside Lilith. She nodded at Whit. "It's hard to believe she dislikes it."

Lilith smiled. "Lucky for you she returned from Elysium when she did. I was getting ready to position *you* for next year's election."

Cimbri laughed. "Gaea! Zoe's antics must have been making you desperate."

"Crazed," Lilith agreed. "Can you imagine? A huge 'expeditionary force' sent into Elysium? It would have been the start of total war. Vengeance is a thirst that is never quenched."

Cimbri looked around the room. "Where is Captain Ference? I haven't seen her."

Lilith leaned closer. "I wonder if she will come. Last night her trial concluded. Branwen did an able job in Zoe's defense, but the Council still found Zoe guilty of abusing a prisoner in custody. They suspended her from active duty, made her turn in her weapons."

"She will grow dangerous, now," Cimbri warned. "I know you think I'm over-reacting, Lilith, but believe me, Zoe is obsessed with bringing Kali to some sort of 'justice.' Did you hear that Zoe threatened her in the marketplace?"

"Whit didn't report it."

"I doubt if Whit knows," Cimbri returned. "This is tavern gossip from Nakotah. A few days back Zoe followed Amelia through the streets, challenging her to battle. They say Amelia ignored her, kept trading her baskets and herbs, even though Zoe went so far as to strike her, once."

"Amelia half-believes Zoe's accusations," Lilith sighed.

"Then she's the only one who does. In fact, the whole city is talking about The Fall, again, debating what might have happened. The latest idea seems to be that someone framed Maat. They're all waiting for Kali to remember the name of the traitor."

Lilith nodded, thinking about Kali. The young woman had grown fretful, had confessed to Lilith that she felt a deep, inexplicable guilt. *Over what?* Lilith wondered.

"Has she remembered any more?" Cimbri quizzed.

Lilith thought. "Odd things. She plays cello again, passionately, as Kali used to do. She can read both musical notes and written words, but she cannot remember that last year at Isis. She gets right up to the day she won her corporal stripes, then becomes—well—panicky. When Amelia starts pacing or clutching her hair, Whit takes her off for some distraction."

Cimbri stroked her chin. "And the nightmares?"

"As you predicted, they have subsided. Whit says that she often wakes to find Amelia crying, but it is from memories, now, not dreams. She mourns her mother, her friends."

Cimbri reached out, held her hand. "Many of us cry at night. The mind-bond brought the past to life."

They both looked across the hall to where Amelia stood with Nakotah, sampling brews at the beer-tasting table. The pale blue bodysuit Amelia wore accented her bright hair. Amelia had hardly finished a sampling cup, when Nakotah handed her another.

Lilith said, "*That* is not what I had in mind when I asked Nakotah to help her re-adjust socially."

Cimbri shook her head. "Nakotah thinks Amelia is in need of some fun."

"The whole colony seems to think Amelia is in need of something," Lilith stated. "My kitchen is overflowing with sumptuous treats. Women come by all day, bringing her things. The outfit she wears tonight is the anonymous gift of some adoring elder. And frankly, Whit is getting annoyed about the lengthy embraces some of the bolder ones seem compelled to bestow."

Cimbri smiled in Whit's direction. "She knows her good fortune. She worries that Kali may not like her as much as Amelia does."

Whit saw the smile and began excusing herself, trying to make her way through the admirers.

"Are not Kali and Amelia the same woman?" Lilith asked, suddenly realizing that Cimbri had made a valid point.

"That is what we all wait to discover," Cimbri answered, her eyes still on the tall, dark woman, resplendent in her uniform.

Whit joined them, muttering, "Please don't ask me about controlling urban growth or when we will re-tool the sewage-fertilization units!"

Cimbri brushed a piece of lint from the burgundy jacket. "A mere escape from Elysium, the rescue of a fair maiden and they think you can fix anything."

Whit replied, "The maiden rescued me and as for fixing things—just look at my tie!" She pulled awkwardly at the western string tie that held her shirt collar closed.

Cimbri stepped closer and created a perfect, loopy bow.

Lilith watched Whit look over Cimbri's head impatiently, searching the crowd for another face. Cimbri glanced up, noted Whit's inattention and quickly stepped away from her.

The musicians broke into a lively reel and the crowd became a mass of stomping boots and swirling skirts. Lilith saw Nakotah steer Amelia into the revelers, obviously teaching her dance steps. Amelia's face was flushed, whether from the beer-tasting or the activity, Lilith wasn't sure, but the haunted look was gone and Lilith blessed Nakotah for that.

Nakotah held Amelia a little tighter than necessary after a well-executed twirl. Cimbri remarked, "I think it's about time to break that up," and moved into the crowd.

Whit agreed laughingly, and began to follow her, then hesitated. She turned to Lilith to be sure she was all right.

"I have been alone at many a harvest celebration, Whit. Go enjoy the evening."

And then Lilith sat watching the flirting and dancing. She watched delightedly as Nakotah put Cimbri through a series of intricate moves, ending in a dip in Nakotah's arms. Meanwhile, Whit and Amelia moved slowly together, lost in a haze of intimacy that had little to do with the beat of the music.

Lilith noticed Branwen standing alone at the edge of the dancers, her intense stare leveled on Whit and Amelia. *Now what's that all about?* Lilith wondered. *Bran told me weeks ago that she's not interested in Whit.*

Styx sat down in the chair Cimbri had vacated, draping her large hand over Lilith's and giving a perfunctory squeeze in greeting.

Lilith felt surprised; she had never seen Styx dressed so well. A bodysuit on well-rounded Cimbri or svelte Amelia was pleasing; however, seeing an older woman like Styx carry off the clinging black so well was...rather inspirational.

Lilith nodded. "A magnificent Kern Supper this year." She tried to withdraw her hand but Styx wouldn't let her.

"The shared ordeal of the mind-bond," Styx agreed. "It will unite the community for many seasons to come."

Lilith waited, puzzled, sure Styx was not finished.

The Mexican face looked troubled. "I knew, even in the midst of it, that something more was going to occur for you. Something beyond the rending horror the rest of us were experiencing. Then I felt your very bones cry out when you saw Maat in the fire."

Lilith turned from her, the nausea all-encompassing. She had known how Maat had died, but *seeing* it, *seeing* it had been...ghastly.

Styx sighed. "You have never stopped loving her."

Lilith covered her face with her hand. The music, the heavy scents of perfume and food were suddenly too much. She wanted to leave.

"Please don't run from me, Lilith. I have waited years to speak to you."

Lilith took a deep breath and looked at the woman. High cheekbones and weather-etched planes on a bronze face—a face she had known since childhood.

Styx solemnly looked back at her. "When our sister city Isis fell, you supported us, led us, even healed us. We have elected you Leader many times now, and you have served us well—too well. You have ignored your own needs for too long.

"You had begun that denial of self long before Isis fell. Your heart grew a shell after Maat. You denied yourself love, the Goddess's greatest gift. You are far more skilled at blocking the path to your heart than Whitaker ever managed."

Lilith stared at her, stunned. *Who does she think she is? I am no child to be lectured to and...*Styx broke into her thoughts. "I can see denied lust in a woman like an eagle sees trout in a lake. I have always desired you, Lilith. I long to feed you, body and soul."

Lilith wavered. She felt absolutely mesmerized by those direct, devouring eyes. After years of bored security, it seemed...beguilingly tempting.

"Come with me." Styx urged, standing up and tugging her upright.

Lilith glanced around at the crowd. No one was even noticing this encounter. Everyone was involved in their own conversations, their own intrigues.

"Come, Lilith. Please."

It was the hoarse need in the whisper that immersed her. Lilith found herself being led from the room.

*****

Amelia leaned against Whit, luxuriating in the warm, solid body that embraced her. The hall had grown darker, the music slower and this heady sensation of moving together was undoing her. She felt the air change, become damp and cool. She lifted her head from Whit's shoulder and discovered they were on the wooden deck that surrounded the Artemis Cedar House.

Whit kept an arm around her waist, pulling her across the planks to the staircase. Down they went, then across the road, down the street. Amelia heard footsteps and glanced back. A small figure darted into the shadow of a doorway. When she looked over her shoulder again, the street was empty.

The two lovers ran down the wooden steps, onto the beach, then stood together, entranced.

The moon rose in the late October sky overhead, turning the wind-sculpted waters of the Sound into liquid silver. The beach sand was a wet, glistening width between the street lights of the city and the wash of the tide. Amelia shivered in the cut of the wind.

Suddenly Whit was kissing her, warming her. Whit backed her up against the granite rocks of the tide wall, the hands steadily searching, commanding her surrender.

Then, all at once, Whit faltered. She grasped Amelia, pulled her into a fierce embrace, murmuring, "I love you."

"I love you," Amelia answered, smiling.

Whit stepped away from her, breathing quickly. "I—I can be black with moods, mean-tempered, selfish. You may find other women more to your liking."

Amelia looked at her, saw the fear in her eyes, heard it in the slight quaver of her voice. Whit, who was afraid of nothing, was afraid of this—deeply, terribly afraid.

Whit rushed on, "I must return to my farm. Friends have been tending it for me, but...I have to go back soon."

"Maybe I could help you," Amelia offered.

"You are newly returned to the community. I'm sure you want to be near Lilith. She's your family. And there is so much to do here in Artemis."

"I want to be with *you*," Amelia stated, daring to be firmer this time.

Whit paused, then relief broke across her face. "You do?"

"Of course!" Amelia laughed, mildly exasperated.

They laughed together, embraced, leaned into each other.

After taking a deep breath, Whit whispered in her ear, "I'm asking you to be my partner."

"I thought so," Amelia remarked, then sighed, "Yes."

"Yes?"

"Is this for life?" Amelia demanded.

Whit pulled back and looked into her eyes. *"Yes!"*

"Good."

Whit came at her, moving her back against the sea wall, consuming her with hands and mouth. Rapidly, Amelia was aflame with pleasure, writhing helplessly beneath Whit's skilled touch.

And then a voice cut the night, commanding, "Get away from the Elysian, Major."

Return to Isis

*****

Cimbri walked thoughtfully along the street in the moon-bright night. At last she remarked, "I think you've insulted me."

Beside her, Nakotah strode, hands in her pockets. She shrugged. "I'll spend the night with you when you're doing it for the right reason."

Cimbri walked faster. "And just what reason am I supposed to be using, now?"

"You're trying to get over Whit's rejection."

Cimbri whirled. "What?! *I* rejected *Whit*, two years ago!"

Nakotah sighed. "And you've been flirting with her, tormenting the poor woman since she came back from Elysium. Everyone has seen it, Cimbri."

Cimbri started off again, livid.

Nakotah kept up with her. "But first you went after Kali, didn't you?"

"Oh! You are impossible!"

"I saw you that day you and Whit took her round to the shops. You were casting for her—admit it. But Kali was not the innocent you all seem to remember her as. She had already been played like a trout on a line, and knew a shiny lure when she saw one. Whit was much better bait."

Cimbri stopped, seizing Nakotah by the arm of her warrior's jacket. "End the fish story! What do you know about Kali?"

Nakotah elaborated, "For a short time, I bunked next to Kali in the warrior's barracks at Isis. She had an affair. For months, just before The Fall, she would slip through the window in the middle of the night. It was a high-ranking politician, much older than she, and Kali's first woman. She was crazed with it—heartsick half the time and hungering the rest. The Security Squad finally arrested her as she came back one night."

"Go on!" Cimbri urged.

"The trial was a monkey court. Kali made no defense, the lover never revealed herself. Kali was found guilty of abandoning her post—much worse than being 'away without leave.' Maat was trying to break her and I know why! The mysterious older woman was no mystery to me!

"Kali had latrine duty, laundry detail, kitchen muck-out by day, round the clock guard duty each night. After a few weeks, she ended up in the infirmary because she started passing out. But she never complained. Little brat that I was, I went to see Maat—told her she was being unfair—then I was transferred to Artemis so fast that my head spun. And Kali told me off about it before I left. Kali said she had been a fool, said she deserved the harsh treatment.

"And that's why the warriors are so eager to claim her as one of them. Because even at fourteen, she was a woman."

Cimbri watched Nakotah toss her head, vehement as she spoke the last words. The blue-black mane of thick hair rose from her shoulders and fell over to her back. Cimbri felt an electric charge shoot through her. Nakotah was really rather magnificent when she was like this. What would she be like hot and wet between the sheets?

"And I am not a woman?" Cimbri asked, sensing somehow, that she was being criticized by comparison.

The black eyes slowly moved over her, head to foot. Nakotah said, "You are a woman who loves with her body but not with her soul. I will have both or neither. The real question is, are you brave enough to take such a risk?"

Cimbri broke the gaze, feeling as if all the oxygen had suddenly left the cool night air around her. She was stunned that Nakotah had seen her weakness, her fear of emotional intimacy. There would be no quick, zesty autumn affair with this one. Nakotah was after a relationship.

There was a sound of scuffling feet. A harsh voice ordered, "Hurry up!"

Cimbri and Nakotah both turned and saw three figures move from the cross-street into the intersection before them. Two women walked in front; another, smaller woman walked behind them—holding something, pointing something—at their backs. When the threesome passed under a street lamp, Cimbri recognized the long-legged walk before she recognized the dress uniform.

"It's Whit," Cimbri remarked in a perfectly normal voice. The blonde woman next to her had to be Amelia. Cimbri opened her mouth to say so and Nakotah clamped a hand over her lips.

Outraged by such treatment, Cimbri grabbed the warrior's wrist, tried to struggle free.

"Shh," Nakotah whispered urgently. "Zoe has a gun on them."

A gun? Cimbri stared at the women who were already through the intersection, disappearing into the side street.

"I think they're heading to the airfield." Nakotah pushed Cimbri, whispering, "Go get help." Nakotah stepped away, intent on action, the warrior part of her emerging quickly.

Curious, Cimbri trailed her into the intersection. Movement caught the corner of Cimbri's eye. Another woman was following right behind them. She turned to see who it was.

White light. The flash stung like a hundred bee stings. Cimbri dropped, groaning. She realized Nakotah was right next to her, lying very still. There was another flash of light, farther away, then hushed voices. Cimbri lay there, stunned, listening to the clatter of boots running away.

— 12 —

Lilith leaned against the kitchen table and poured the brew. Styx took a dutiful sip, contemplating her over the cup.

How did I get into this? Lilith asked herself. It had been years since she had engaged in this sort of elaborate, casual charade. All it had taken was one gentle kiss at the door and Lilith had invited her in. All it would take now was a touch at the right moment and the woman would be in her bed.

Lilith cut a glance at the distinctive, high-cheeked face. Historian, psychic, fiftyish, eccentric. The young warriors called her "Trashpicker" because she was constantly gathering artifacts, dragging the refuse back to warehouses no one visited. She knew the ruins of Seattle, farther down the Sound, as well as she knew the streets of Artemis. The woman lived more in the past than in the present.

"The past has value, too," Styx murmured.

Lilith nearly dropped her cup.

Styx shrugged. "You ponder pretty loud."

Lilith stared, unnerved.

Styx stared back. "You have a bit of the gift, too, or I could never hear you."

Lilith admitted, "I spent a few years with Baubo, developing intuitive sensitivity."

"You employed it well as a pilot, if not in daily life."

Lilith flared, "I knew about Maat, if that's what you mean. Every time I left Artemis on a grain trade I knew Maat and that woman..." Lilith caught herself. She took a deep breath, turned away from the level gaze.

"The scar still aches," Styx said.

Lilith swung back, sputtering, "What do you know about a love like that? You spent your youth following Baubo, the only celibate in Freeland, the two of you cloistered away like Medieval nuns! Even after Baubo disappeared, you went on meditating, fasting, wandering."

Styx disarmed her completely by laughing. "If you want to know, ask," Styx prompted.

Lilith frowned. "How could you live like that?"

"I was waiting for the one I wanted," Styx said, reaching out and holding her hand. "And you weren't ready, then."

Lilith closed her eyes. Disbelief flooded her, she shook her head, denying.

*****

Cimbri breathed another lungful of air into Nakotah, kneeled back and pushed down on the sternum. She was growing dizzy. If no one came soon...once again she cried out, calling for help. Tears were wet on her face. The refrain, "Please don't die, please don't die," echoed in her head, a mantra in the moonlight. She forced another breath past cool lips, felt icy panic clawing free of her self-control.

Far in the distance, she could hear joyful music and crowd noise. All of Artemis was celebrating and Nakotah was dying here in the street. Goddess knew what was happening to Whit and Amelia and still no one came! She heard a roar. A huge grain transport ship lifted over her head, then arced toward the water. The night went back to distant music and laughter.

Time seemed to wrap close around her chest, squeezing her into nothingness. Cimbri clung to her measured pattern, blowing breath into Nakotah, concentrating on the count.

And then at last someone pushed her aside. There were suddenly women all around her, smoothly taking over the C.P.R. During the avalanche of questions, Cimbri lay her head on the street stones and began to cry.

*****

The ship banked sharply. Amelia rolled across the dark cargo hold, choking on grain dust. She slammed into a molded metal wall. The wild ride was beginning to hurt. She tried to flex strength back to her limbs. The ship tipped to the opposite side.

A limp form slid into her, the scent of the skin so recognizable. Whit didn't seem to be conscious, but she herself was only half-awake. She couldn't think straight, yet, couldn't evaluate much.

Was it Cimbri she had seen? From the shadows down the street had come the bright burst of a sedation gun. Whit had whirled on Zoe, ready to fight. All Amelia remembered was a white light.

Her sluggish mind finally churned up the meaning. Zoe had shot them with a sedation gun! The swell of rage carried some energy through her body.

Whit rolled away, then rolled back and collided with her. By sheer force of will Amelia dug her hands into the back of Whit's breeches. They continued to drift from side to side and Amelia focused her soupy brain on protecting Whit from the walls.

*****

The engine had cut off. Amelia lay half-awake, unable to disengage from her grip on Whit. After what seemed like a long time, the cargo door slid open. Amelia was face down, twisted against Whit's side, unable to get a look at the figures hovering over her.

"She's got a good hold on that ass," Zoe scoffed.

"Separate them," a quiet, firm voice replied.

Zoe peeled Amelia's fingers from Whit's breeches. Amelia managed to curse her.

"She's talking!" Zoe hissed. "She's not even supposed to be conscious! I had the weapon at two thirds power!"

Smooth, self-assured, the other voice said, "I thought as much. You're so emotional over this you may end up killing her, yet. I told you to chain them in the flight cabin and I find them in here. You very nearly damaged my cargo, Captain. I need them alive."

"But how is she awake?!" Zoe sounded angry. She obviously didn't like being chastised in front of Amelia. "I made sure she got most of the blast, yet Whitaker's out and *she's* talking!"

"You sound like the Regs when she escaped them—the idiots—putting it down to witchcraft instead of science. Her adrenaline kicks in and negates the dosage. Natural resistance. She inherited it from Maat."

"What?" Zoe demanded.

"Body chemistry. We all have our peculiar weaknesses and strengths. And there is a wealth of secrets in the juice of this lovely peach."

A hand came against Amelia's cheek. She stiffened, alarms going off deep in her mind. There was something in that expression, "this lovely peach." She had heard it before, she had heard that voice say it before.

"Then...she did escape?" Zoe asked, her voice different. There was shock in the tone.

There was a long, damning silence. Amelia fervently wished she could see their faces.

Zoe whispered, "I thought the mind-bond ended where it did because she collaborated."

"The mind-bond again. How you harp on that! I'm sorry I missed it. I just couldn't risk her knowing me."

I do know her, Amelia thought. The memory was right there at the edge of the mist.

Zoe spoke with anguish. "She escaped. Why her and no one else?"

"The Tribune that led the raid claimed her as a prize and took her back with him. She has that Aryan look they cherish—you know how racist they are. The police insisted on interrogations and she spent a few weeks in a Chicago prison. When the Tribune went to sample her, he was enraged. He wanted more of that Amazon spunk, a little spicy fight before the rape. The police brought him a near-dead zombie.

"The Tribune reasserted his claim, took her out of there and installed her in an expensive whore house. The women nursed her back to some semblance of health, though it's documented that she'd lost the power of speech by then. The Tribune returned one day, apparently intent on some sport. It seems he underestimated her. They found him dead in one of those sound-proof pleasure rooms. Kali had disappeared."

"How do you know all this?" Zoe sounded rather at a loss.

"It's in the Regulator files Whit beamed to Lilith."

"And you never reported it? You didn't tell Lilith?" Zoe was incredulous.

The other voice was contemptuous. "Lilith is only an old grain-swapper. She doesn't know how to rule. She hasn't even noticed that I've taken the MED memory disks that store all that Reg data."

Zoe said, "And Maat? Did she know how to rule?"

No answer.

Zoe again, her voice hard now. "How *did* the Regs get into Freeland?"

"You are in this up to your warrior's badge, Captain—the badge I retrieved for you after Lilith demeaned and disgraced you. Or should I call you Major? After Whitaker's demise we will need another Major. Remember, once Lilith is disposed of, I will rule Artemis." The voice was persuasive, reasonable.

Amelia lay listening to the tone. Who was this woman? Why did she know and welcome and fear that voice?

There was a lengthy silence. Amelia felt her whole body oozing down, dropping lower into the sleep she craved. As long as there was motion or sound she could focus, she could span the wide gaps between conscious moments. Stillness, silence, those were the enemies.

Zoe's shout pulled her out of the void. "It wasn't Maat, *was* it?!"

She heard a strange, plunging thud, a shrill wail. A heavy clunk on metal.

Someone grabbed her shoulder, tugged her over. She saw Zoe lying on the floor, eyes wide, bleeding to death from the wound in her stomach.

Amelia looked up, full into the face of the murderer.

And knew her.

*****

It was near daybreak and Cimbri still watched the instruments anxiously, still evaluated read-outs. Other healers clustered around her, urging her to let them take over.

"I have to monitor the patient's progress," she repeated. She didn't tell them that it was she who was making Nakotah breathe, she who was sending blood through those vessels. She didn't tell them that if she took herself from here and the woman died....

Lilith came up beside her and squeezed her hand.

Cimbri barely glanced at her.

"We've combed Artemis," Lilith said. "No sign of Whit, Amelia or Zoe. How is Nakotah?"

"She's...oh Lilith..." Cimbri was crying uncontrollably before she could say any more.

Lilith held her. Cimbri was barely aware of being guided away. In the office, Lilith settled her on the couch, rocked her.

She cried until sleep slunk in on the edge of the exhausted sobs, slunk in and covered her like a warm blanket. She protested when Lilith lay her down, telling her she didn't have to sleep, just close her eyes for a while. Cimbri made up her mind to go back to Nakotah, but she had already surrendered. She went to Nakotah's side in a dream.

*****

All the warriors in Artemis turned out for the land-air search.

Impatient and anxious, Lilith used her position as Leader to demand first take-off. She declared her intentions across the video communications unit, then put the ship in vertical climb and took her up. "I have no idea where to start," she mused.

Styx sat beside her, engrossed in plotting map coordinates on the computer. "Use your gift."

"I am! All night I've been...reaching. There's nothing. Whit and Amelia are gone, a ship is missing and one of our best warriors is in a coma! Damn Zoe!"

Lilith changed drives and the ship jumped forward, darting away from Artemis. Styx was thrown against her flight chair. Lilith glanced over, apologized, slowed the craft. Styx gave her a wry smile and told her she loved speed. Lilith gave the ship full power.

They raced over the lush countryside, their eyes searching for the glitter of another transport ship. This was not a small conveyance, like the jetcrafts—this was a full sized grain trader. It would be difficult to camouflage, even in the mountains. Lilith knew that finding the ship could be their only chance.

They searched all day, until their eyes felt like they would drop from their sockets. They only saw ships in the air, other searchers who hailed them on the radio channels.

Near twilight, warriors began calling Lilith, the youthful voices discouraged as they reported "no sightings." All the pilots and on-ground searchers were heading home to Artemis. One by one, calls came in from the other colonies, stating that no stray grain ships had been encountered. Lilith responded with her habitual calm reserve, thanking everyone, ordering a resumption of efforts at daylight.

Then she turned off the radio and stared into the sunset. She had not felt such utter despair, such crushing hopelessness since.... Styx turned and sighed, "Since Maat."

Lilith threw a fierce glance at her.

"You're loud," Styx grumbled.

"Stop listening!"

"Too bad someone else didn't listen," Styx said, fidgeting with the video dials. The monitor flicked to the view from the rear camera on the ship. The sky behind them was already a deep, sea-blue of oncoming night.

Lilith aimed the ship due west, brooding. "Where can they be? How could anyone hide that huge grain trader?"

Styx was riveted, staring at the video screen. She increased magnification, pointing at the screen. "Your answer."

Lilith focused on the small object in the sky behind them, feeling exasperated with Styx. It was probably a bird or a spot of dirt on the camera lens. Then came a sight Lilith had seen a thousand times: the dip of a wing catching sunlight. A craft was landing, way up in the Cascades, probably on the landing strip at Isis.

"She's been in the air all along!" Lilith exclaimed. "Zoe must have altered the numbers on the side of the ⁻hip. We've probably been criss-crossing with her all day!" Lilith reached for the radio mike.

Styx knocked her hand away from it. "You'll only alert them! We can't call for help."

"Them?" Lilith had been blaming one person all day. An accomplice had never entered her mind.

"The shot that hit Nakotah—it couldn't have come from Zoe. Zoe was ahead of them. The wound is on the back of Nakotah's head, the mark fan-like—which means a direct hit. Someone else was following Cimbri and Nakotah."

Lilith looked at Styx with renewed respect, then began watching the blip on camera drop below the tree line. "I guess it is up to us, Trashpicker."

Styx nodded, grinning at the name. She killed the inner and outer ship lights, triggered the outer shields into radar-block mode. Lilith watched her, impressed that Styx knew so much about night action.

"Don't be impressed, I'm hearing you again," Styx murmured.

Lilith broke into a belly laugh, the like of which had not overtaken her in many years.

Styx grinned back, then sobered and began revealing other information. "Cimbri was distraught in the street. I couldn't make much sense out of her thoughts, but enough. She told me that Nakotah had been talking about Kali, about a lover Kali had been involved with, years ago. That is the key to this." Styx nodded to herself, obviously satisfied.

"What?" Lilith said. It made no sense to her at all. *What lover? There had been rumors, but....*

"The rumors were true." Styx hiked up her trousers, felt inside her boot. Lilith watched the partial emergence and then disappearance of a knife in a hidden sheath.

"What does a lover have to do with this? It's Zoe. She's convinced herself that Amelia threw in with the Elysians."

"Look, Lil," Styx began patiently. "Just as Nakotah was telling Cimbri about this mysterious, high-ranking official that once played Kali like a trout on a line, Nakotah is shot with a full-strength sedation blast at close range. Cimbri is, on the other hand, left with only minimal ricochet injury. Doesn't that seem odd?"

Lilith reflected. Yes, it was odd. Very odd. "What else did you hear in Cimbri's thoughts?"

As she talked, Styx loaded drug cartridges into a sedation gun, shoved it in a holster. "That Nakotah better live," she muttered. She left her chair and knelt by Lilith, slipping the gunbelt around her generous middle.

They made eye contact. Lilith felt a strength of affection she had not felt in years. This was not maternal, not the way she felt about Cimbri or Whit or Amelia. This was electric, exhilarating and very much unexpected.

Styx clearly registered the sensation. She said softly, firmly, "You better live, too." She moved back to her seat and prepared a gunbelt for herself.

— 13 —

For hours, ever since her senses had cleared, Amelia had been listening to voices on the radio. The warriors were searching for them. They were also searching for Zoe. But so far, no one had mentioned the name of the woman piloting the ship. So far, no one had hailed them, demanding identification. The only time the pilot had spoken all day had been to respond to a request for a weather report.

Does no one even suspect her? Amelia wondered.

Then, all at once, the search was ending. One by one the search parties reported that they were returning to Artemis and the voices on the radio stopped calling each other. The small, dense knot of fear in her stomach began to grow.

The ship was dropping lower, landing. Amelia looked across the aisle. Whit was chained to the seat and gagged, as Amelia was. The glazed gray eyes stayed on her, fighting through the after-effects of sedation. Amelia knew it would take hours for Whit to climb through the stupor of the second blast given them both this morning.

She was on her own.

The knowledge of what their captor had planned for them flooded her mind. She had to get Whit out of this. That was what she had to focus on, the only thing that mattered. She had to save Whit.

The ship was dropping too fast, she thought, leaning to the port side. The pilot was clearly not as skilled as Whit or Lilith. A crashing bump tossed Amelia sideways in her seat. The shackles, hooked to the armrests, checked her instinctive move to protect her head from the wall. She heard the whop of the contact, saw lights swirl before her and then sank into the velvet black beyond them.

*****

"I said carry her. I need you both, dammit."

The woman's voice seemed to come from very far away. At least the scraping cuffs were off—no wonder Amelia had thrown a fit about them—when had they been removed?

She lost her train of thought.

What was it this woman was shrieking at her? Get up? Yes, that was it. Get up.

Whit tried to marshall her muscles to obedience. Pushing herself out of the seat, she stood, swaying, gripping the back of the chair. Her mouth felt like mud had gathered in there. She reached up and tugged, and wonder of wonders, the cloth gag came away in her hand. Her tongue felt better, but she was so thirsty. She tried to ask for water.

Branwen shouted, "Pick Kali up or I'll kill you!"

Befuddled, Whit went down on her knees. Had Branwen really said that? "Water," she rasped.

She closed her eyes and drifted. Something cool and wet washed over her face. Whit looked up and found Branwen above her, handing her a flight canteen. She fumbled for it, couldn't hold it. Branwen came lower and lifted her, guided the drinking straw to her lips. Whit drank greedily, desperate with thirst, nearly choking.

The voice seemed to be in another room. "Ah Whit," she said, "I have waited to see you like this. My big, strong warrior—so helpless." Whit half-smiled, closed her eyes. The pain in her ribs jolted her awake. "I said get up!" Branwen kicked her again.

What is Branwen doing? Why is she yelling? Whit struggled to roll over. The questions quickly receded into the soft and calm cocoon of irrationality that surrounded her.

What is the matter with me? Whit thought, mildly irritated. She couldn't coordinate her limbs. She was on her hands and knees, now, crawling up a flight chair, trying to use it to haul herself upright.

Branwen was next to her, busily unwrapping the chains from the armrests, then re-fastening the shackles on a pair of slender wrists. Whit dragged her eyes from the wrists, up the arms to the face. *Sweet Mother, it's Amelia.* A large egg-like lump rose on the far side of her forehead.

Of course, she'd hit her head when they'd landed. Whit had seen it. Seen it and forgotten it. What was the matter with her that she would forget something like that?

"Get up!" Branwen bellowed. "I'll carry her myself, but I swear if you can't walk, I'll kill you here and now."

Whit knew she meant what she said. With all her strength, Whit groped up the length of the chair. She lurched toward the exit portal, drunken, unsteady, but walking.

*****

"We have to put the ship down quietly. If we're heard they'll probably do something rash," Styx said.

"That means we glide in," Lilith said.

Lilith readied herself. There would be no engine, no retro-jets to cushion the descent. She would have to dodge the huge Douglas Firs that surrounded the tarmac and land on a small airfield that was already crowded by a big grain transport.

Lilith feared it was death they would find down there in the dark, not a landing. Her hand trembled on the stick.

In the dim light of the instrument panel, Styx brought out her amulet, gripped it. A six-pointed star with the dolphin, Lilith knew. "Delphi." In Greek it meant womb. It was the symbol of the matriarchy that was Artemis.

Lilith settled the ship lower.

Whit and Kali were about as close to being her children as she would get in this life. They were not of her womb, but they were most certainly the children of her heart.

In the home she had shared with Maat, Lilith had taken an active part in raising the "Bean Sprout," as they had called her. And then when Kali was eight, Maat had grown restless, had begun spending a great deal of time in the company of a younger woman—Branwen.

By Kali's ninth birthday, Maat had taken herself and the child to Isis. Branwen had moved in with them. Shortly thereafter, Kali had gone from a bright, eager girl to a rebellious scamp. Every report Lilith heard seemed to get a little bit worse, even after Kali had joined the warriors. Maat never did seem to make the connection on that score. Of course, the youngster had been reacting to the loss of stability, the loss of a family. Maat had seemed to take it all as a personal slight. The elders had said scornfully, "Maat can rule a colony, but not her own daughter."

And then she heard that Kali had been caught off base without permission. There was the old story about an affair, though with whom nobody seemed to know. Isis had fallen before....

Oh, who am I kidding?! Maat had told her to mind her own business and so she had. She'd been a coward, afraid to see Maat, afraid to confront her about the girl.

And then there was Whit. When Lilith had first met the rangy, nineteen year old orphan, there had been no sign of the tough warrior Freeland knew now.

She had heard that Whit was going to drop out of the Agri-Science program, that the young woman was drowning in survivor's guilt. An avid student, Whit had stayed in Artemis that weekend, the weekend Isis had burned, to work on a special project. In the space of a few hours, she had lost her mother, her sisters, her friends. Lilith had already made up her mind to live the rest of her life alone and then, a week after The Fall, she had seen Whit sitting on a bench outside the Cedar House. The grief on that youthful face had ended Lilith's self-absorption. Walking over to Whit, Lilith reached down and took Whit by the hand, home to live with her, to care for her.

Whit, too, had become a daughter. Beneath the gruff exterior, Whit was a delicate soul, full of loving impulses and considerate thoughts. And Lilith had needed Whit, as much as Whit had needed her.

She loved her daughters. They were in need of the best she could manifest tonight.

Lilith carefully threaded the transport down. She could see nothing in the total darkness that hid the land below.

Goddess give me luck, she thought. *Let the wind catch the wings. Let the other ship be out of the way. Let that old seat-of-the-pants-razzle-dazzle get the craft down in one piece.*

She cut the engine.

The wind took them.

*****

Amelia came to, smelling the frosty air. When she lifted her head, the person carrying her slung her off. There were two people, black outlines against the blaze of stars in the sky.

"Can you walk?" It was Branwen.

Amelia got to her feet. "Yes." She knew the answer Branwen wanted to hear. The part of her that was Kali was growing stronger.

"Hi." The other silhouette stumbled toward her.

Whit. Thank the Goddess, Whit was still alive! She grasped her, pulled her close.

Branwen snapped, "Break it up and get moving!"

Whit's slurred voice asked, "Where're we goin?"

"Maat's lab. I've got some unfinished business to attend to there," Branwen replied.

Amelia held Whit's arm, her brain racing through the maze Branwen had designed, trying to find some clarity.

"Lead the way, Kali. Just pretend you're fourteen."

"Washe shayin?" Whit whispered.

"Shh. It's an old game," Amelia soothed. The remorse rushed through her. How could it be that this dark shame, so long unremembered, could be just as powerful, just as bitter?

She started off across the meadow. Whit lurched along, rubber-legged beside her.

From behind them, the smooth voice said, "That's right, keep moving. We don't want anyone to get hurt. This will all be over by morning."

Whit leaned on her, a heavy, reeling weight. Amelia's head ached. She was terribly thirsty, she was cold, she was hungry. The shackles jingled on her hands and feet, shortening her natural stride, tripping her. She lurched through the dark meadow toward the Cedar House and could think of no escape.

Branwen didn't fool her. Branwen could care less if anyone got hurt. Whit was here for a purpose: to insure that Branwen got what she wanted. Amelia would sooner or later give up the codex. She would be forced to exchange information for Whit's safety. And then Branwen would be on her way and they would both be dead.

Finally, she remembered it. All of it. Long ago, Branwen had been the Freeland end of a profitable Black Market. Computer parts, grain, salt, even the precious plastic sedation guns—had been funneled to Elysium each time Branwen crossed the Border. Branwen had acquired a secret stash of gold that was inconceivable in Freeland, where wealth was equated with avarice. As always, since time eternal, small, discreet gifts of gold carried extensive rewards in a community. Branwen had bought her way to power.

The codex—the self-regulating software program that kept the Border in place—had been kept in the Cedar House. In constant contact with the satellites in space, the codex was loaded in a computer and hidden in a vault beneath Maat's laboratory.

Considered priceless, the codex had been protected with four different security barriers. One, the 24-hour-a-day guard posted by the outer door. Two, the building force field that snapped on at any attempted violation of the outer building. Three, the DNA plate that locked Maat's lab. Four, the DNA plate that locked the vault door.

Amelia *knew* it was still there, safe behind Maat's carefully constructed security system. Maat and her unique chemical code were long gone, but there was still one code left, one code that could key the DNA plates. Kali and Branwen both knew about Maat's obsession with back-ups.

And they both knew that Kali was the second key.

Branwen intended to steal the codex and sell it to the Regs for a fabulous sum. The woman walking behind her was willing to unleash Armageddon on Freeland—for money, for power.

Amelia began to shake. Oh, she knew this woman.

Kali. She had been Kali then.

She remembered a rainy December evening. She had gone to the laboratory to show her mother the corporal's stripes she had earned. Her mother had been absorbed in research, had barely looked up from the electron microscope. On the couch her mother had kept in the lab for napping, Kali had fallen asleep, waiting for her mother's attention. When she woke she was disappointed to find that her mother had left a note for her, had gone off to a Council Meeting—as usual, too busy to see her.

She had joined the warriors because she wanted to be like Lil, because she missed Lil, missed the honest, straight-forward way of life they had all shared in Artemis. But her mother had first cheated on Lil, then left her. Maat had fallen in with the charmers, had become vain and ambitious. Kali had begun to hate her for breaking up their family.

Sitting alone in the dark lab, watching the rain coursing down the plexiglass windows, Kali was feeling sorry for herself. Branwen, the new woman who lived in their house and shared her mother's bed, had knocked insistently on the laboratory door. Kali's DNA code could release the lock; Branwen's could not. She didn't think of it then, but it was a measure of which one of them her mother trusted.

She had let Branwen inside, figuring she was there on some errand for her mother. She had gone back to the couch, back to watching the rain.

She remembered looking up and finding Branwen staring at her. The woman had come slowly toward her. It had surprised her when Branwen sat down so close. She was reed thin, there had been plenty of room on the couch, no need to touch. But the touching had only just begun.

"This lovely peach," Branwen had crooned, "is ripe for plucking." Hands had moved across her small chest, slowly strayed up and down the length of her thighs. The shock had gradually given way to an urgent need. The need had given way to a savage want.

Branwen had gazed at her, savoring the power she had over her. She had asked her, softly, over and over, if she liked it and Kali had finally said yes. Her reward for that answer had been unspeakably delicious.

And then Branwen had taught her about physical ecstasy and spiritual torment. In the months that followed, Branwen had rendered her mindless with lust, had teased her into many, many other sessions in the laboratory.

As Kali lay on the couch, her mind would tell her that this was wrong, that she was breaking the warrior code of honor. She was acutely aware that Branwen was twenty years older than her, that Branwen was her mother's woman. But the guilt was not enough to keep her from climbing through the barrack's window at night. It was not enough to keep her from dancing on Branwen's fingers. The sex only seemed to get more intense, more wild when she tried to resist it.

And then the whole thing had slid into domination and submission. Branwen overpowering her, tying her hands, Branwen whispering, "I own you," in her ear as she came.

When Branwen approached her, she trembled. When Branwen stroked her, she lost all reason. And whenever Branwen wanted, she met her again in guilty secrecy.

Then the Security Squad arrested her, took her to the Brig. The officer-in-charge had stood outside the force field, watching Kali pace the containment room, as they both waited for Maat.

"Have you figured it out, yet? Do you know who turned you in?" the officer had laughed.

Kali had kept on pacing, horrified that it had come to this, that she had let herself go so far—all for the touch of a woman that she half-hated.

The officer had said, "Branwen Evans, Isis Council member, filed the complaint. Probably called it in just after you had left her...attentions."

Dumbfounded, Kali had stopped pacing, had stared at the woman. She had felt as if a grain transport had fallen out of the sky, onto her head.

The officer had told her, "Don't worry, your secret dies with me. You're not the first she's driven crazy. Last year, I was the one she conquered."

Later, Maat arrived. For hours, her mother had railed at her, demanding to know why she had abandoned her post. Kali swore to herself that the least she could do was protect Maat from the sordid truth. Maat would find out sooner or later that Branwen was an opportunist. No woman needed her daughter to expose an unworthy partner.

And so at last they had confined her to base, slapped endless details on her. And she had done them willingly, needing to do penance for what felt so dirty and incestuous. She found she could barely meet her mother's eyes on the rare occasions when they crossed paths. After that, she simply refused to look at Branwen altogether.

Remembering all this was so painful; it hurt—physically hurt. Her skull felt ready to crack in half, but Amelia persisted in prodding the tender, hazy recollections, looking for more.

Two months later, Branwen had gone into Elysium on a standard undercover operation. After returning through the Bordergate, Branwen had made a radio report, saying she would be stopping in Artemis. And then all flaming hell had arrived at Isis.

Just before the Elysian's attacked, Kali had been standing guard at the Cedar House. Maat had locked up the lab and then coldly saluted her as she passed through the huge outer door.

She had next seen her mother at the stake, in flames.

She staggered with the thought of it. She was shaking all over now, sick and cold and so tired. *That's enough! Stop remembering*, she told herself.

The Tribune's voice was speaking to her. "Are you listening to me, Little One?"

The internal fog closed in, curling like a live thing. *Don't remember*, she told herself. This was bad, she could feel it, smell it....

The man-smell assaulted her. She was in a room with him, a naked man. He was telling her that Branwen had made a bargain with them. Branwen had told them of the codex. As he spoke, the man was undressing her. She was standing before him, very still, very docile. They had "trained" her to be feminine for him—to look down, shut up, become a post for him to ogle and hump. But she was enraged, her ears were pounding with hot blood. She'd been afraid for so long, but now there was only fury.

He had left the ceremonial sword—the sword he had won by laying waste to Isis—across the room beside his neatly folded clothing. He was telling her that she'd better cooperate, better tell them how the Bordergates worked, before she ended up like her mother. Something inside her....

The bright stars above swung into focus as her mind scuttled back, away from the memory. *What am I so afraid of? What happened?*

The memory came roaring back. The Tribune was laughing—imitating the way her mother had gone up in flames, the way she had twisted, screaming. Something inside Kali shattered, exploded, like a fir tree hit by lightning.

She was dashing across the room, seizing the sword and turning. He was right behind her, the laughter gone, disbelief flooding his eyes.

On sheer body memory and fury, she was unleashing a classic Freeland warrior sword attack. Slice, feint, slice, stab. The Tribune was quickly backing up, a small scream coming from him as he realized she could really use this weapon and he would never get the door unlocked fast enough to escape. And then she was chopping him like a cornstalk, axing him near in half. Blood—spurting from his mouth, his nose. She was slashing him again and again, yelling with triumph, like the Regs had yelled at Isis.

I'm going to be sick.

She was on her knees. Branwen was shouting at her. The dry retching went into spasms.

Stop remembering, she thought wearily, uselessly.

She didn't want to remember, she wanted it all to leave her. As a matter of fact, dying was becoming an attractive alternative to this. She wouldn't mind so much dying tonight.

Branwen was pulling her up, hissing threats.

Maybe she could go on the attack, trick Branwen into killing her. No, Branwen would just get mad, and then kill Whit, too. If only she could get Whit out of here.

But Whit was leaning against the large wooden door of the Cedar House, oblivious to the danger. Amelia could actually hear her humming.

Feeling utterly defeated, Amelia began to weep.

*****

Cimbri surveyed the warriors who had abruptly left their homes, their meals, their baths to return to the airfield. Their normally smart gray uniforms were askew, some buttoned wrong, some badly wrinkled. Gunbelts usually worn around their waists were slung over shoulders. They had gotten her distress call and had plainly come as fast as they could.

She had never had much time for the warriors, had thought them too proud and masculine and arrogant. It had been the carefully disguised shyness that had drawn her to Whit, not the fact that the woman was beloved by a bunch of modern day butches. It was the devilish child in Nakotah that Cimbri found irresistible, not the haughty warrior's demeanor.

As a matter of fact, Cimbri had thought herself better than these women. After all, they cultivated brawn, honed the ability to fight—and who needed that sort of thing in a civilized age?

She had been stupid. She knew it now.

They were all warriors, all the women of Artemis, whether in uniform or not. Just as all the women of Isis had been warriors, and had proven it with their resistance unto death. With their DNA codes, any one of the women who burned in that field could have opened the door to the Cedar House. Instead, they had withheld the information, had allowed the Regs to uselessly hammer at the door, until the Regs had tripped the building force field. The women of Isis had died together, silent, united.

Cimbri watched the last few warriors running across the tarmac, hair disheveled, faces tired.

It wasn't about male and female, she thought. In the heterosexual Freeland colonies, the alarm was going up, the warriors were gathering, the ships were being re-charged, re-fueled, just like here. A Freelandian Leader had disappeared. The country was rallying.

This was what old America had aspired to be hundreds of years ago, before justice and freedom had become the province of rich, white men.

Cimbri looked at them, roughly four hundred of them, shifting quietly, waiting for her to speak. They would go to their deaths for what they believed in, for ideals, for love of each other.

Tears sprang into her eyes. Making her voice loud enough to carry, she said, "Lilith and Styx have not returned."

Above the responding clamor, someone demanded, "Who saw them last?"

"They were following Green River, heading west," came the answer.

"Who's in command?" someone else said.

"Where's Branwen? She's Co-leader. Isn't it time she showed up?"

"She was on the radio earlier," a young, brash one said. "She flew a ship in the search."

"She did not," a mechanic retorted. "She never logged a flight plan."

A confusing chorus of agreement and dissension ensued. Cimbri watched them sorting it out, a centipede that had lost its head. She was just about to lose her newly discovered good opinion of them, when someone stepped forward and roared at them all to shut up.

It was Griffin, Nakotah's best friend. She was a lieutenant, not the highest rank among them, but she had a plan.

— 14 —

Lilith glanced at the three dimensional gauges and then concentrated on keeping the ship's nose up. She knew, just *knew* that the tree line had ended. She dipped the transport abruptly lower. They coasted. Lilith sent her every psychic awareness antennae out like so many invisible tentacles. Just before they hit the earth, she understood that they were nowhere near the landing strip.

Amazingly, they jounced only once, then skidded freely across bumpy, spongy terrain. At long last they stopped. The ship was absorbed in thick night-quiet.

Lilith blew out the breath she'd been holding.

"Never even scraped a rock," Styx said in wonder.

Lilith released the seat restraint, left the cockpit chair, felt her way to the exit portal. A peek through the window showed her that they were in the meadow before the Isis Cedar House.

Styx clambered after her. "That was the best damn flying I've ever seen!" she crowed in a hoarse whisper.

Styx grabbed Lilith's shoulders, spun her into an about-face. The kiss that followed rocked Lilith. For an instant she thought she heard the proverbial bells ringing, then realized it was no fantasy.

Styx stepped away, listening too. "Bells?"

"The Cedar House," Lilith said. "It's probably about as close as Amelia can get to sending up a flare."

*****

"Get away from that thing!" Branwen yelled.

Whit shoved herself off the carillon keyboard and another series of chimes pealed out. She dropped her head back, trying to see what she knew was there in the dark tower. They sounded so pretty, so...loud.

Loud? Loud was good. She and Amelia were in trouble—she knew that much. She dropped her hand to the keys and set them off again.

The blow in the stomach doubled her over.

"Leave her alone!" Amelia cried.

Something struck the back of her head. Whit hit the floor and stayed there.

Branwen said contemptuously, "She should have been taken by the Regs. Then, you and your shredded little memory would have stayed in Elysium."

Amelia knelt by Whit, a cheerless enlightenment in her eyes. "*You* reported her to the Regs, the way you once reported me to the Security Squad. You are truly a worm, Branwen," she said under her breath.

Whit struggled to breathe. Her stomach muscles were frozen with the force of the blow given her, as was her mind with what she'd just heard. *Branwen turned me into the Regs? Was that what Amelia said?*

Trying hard to focus, Whit recognized the room. They were in the large chamber beyond the Council Room. Maat's lab was behind the nearest door.

Serene and self-assured, Branwen stood over them, wearing green camouflage clothing. *Is she on a mission?* Whit thought fuzzily.

"You see, Kali, I had to end the affair," Branwen was saying with remorse. "Your mother was getting suspicious. You were so young, so transparent, Kali."

Amelia recoiled from the hand against her cheek, said fiercely, "It was *you* who sabotaged all the Border caches."

As the sharp pain receded, Whit felt herself go unanchored again. She was floating, sleepy. Then, there were hands in her hair. She looked up and smiled at Amelia, but Amelia didn't smile back. The brown eyes were rimmed with tears. Whit watched Branwen grab Amelia's arms from behind and haul her to her feet.

Branwen's voice was odd. "I couldn't believe it when I realized it was you."

The distressed, brown eyes stayed on Whit. *She's telling me something*, Whit thought.

"It wasn't until we reached Artemis," Branwen admitted, "and Zoe put the shackles on you. You were gaunt, haggard with fever, but when you struggled I saw...that spirit. I have always loved you for it, Kali."

Amelia seemed stricken.

Branwen looked as if she were feeding off the discomfort she was causing.

"You never loved me," Amelia replied softly.

Branwen ignored the remark, slowly caressed the pale blue bodysuit that fitted Amelia like skin. "Since your recuperation I have had no doubt. You're taller, more comely than ever. The Great Maat was but a stepping-stone for me. You were the unexpected little gem in that household. I nearly lost it all in my craving for you."

Amelia sidled away from her, yanked against the shackles.

"I never meant to hurt you," Branwen continued, reaching out and stroking Amelia's shoulder.

Through a haze, it came to Whit that Branwen was playing Amelia, as Branwen had often played the Council, to get her way. It was a skill she had finely tuned over the years. She was a master at subtle manipulation.

Branwen explained, "Before my last trip into Elysium, Maat told me to move out of the Leader's House. She had...searched my belongings...found things...."

"Like a few sacks of gold the Elysians gave you?" Amelia asked, the deep bitterness surfacing.

"She threatened me, Kali. I couldn't allow her to...You know what she was like—so overbearing and inflexible!"

"And so you betrayed an entire city?" Amelia asked, her voice breaking.

"I had to!"

Tears rolling down, Amelia shook her head. She gazed at the stone statue that stood nearby.

Whit followed her eyes. The Burned Ones, the grotesque artwork that caught in hard reality what had happened in the meadow beyond the outer door. She remembered that not long ago Amelia had come into this room and faced that depiction of horror alone. Seeing those contorted faces, those writhing figures, had been the push that had brought the memories out of the nightmares and into the waking day.

"So many died," Amelia choked. "Bran, how could you *do* that to us?"

In a perfectly reasonable voice, Branwen said, "She who controls the Border, controls both Freeland and Elysium. It is the ultimate power. Maat wouldn't give me access to the software. I simply had to have access. I had to have the power."

Amelia's shoulders sagged. "You're mad."

"Oh, no. I know how to rule, how to get things done, how to make a profit. That's not madness."

Amelia yelled, "You're right! You're not mad, just depraved, Branwen!" Amelia turned away, overcome with helpless anger and loathing.

Like a beast, Branwen's beautiful face changed. Whit watched her move behind Amelia and pounce. Hands slipped under Amelia's arms and gripped each breast, yanking Amelia into a tight embrace. Branwen roughly mauled the front of her, then lowered her head, bit Amelia's neck. A hand slid down to Amelia's crotch.

Amelia was struggling to fling her off, but her movements were clumsy and slow.

She's been drugged, Whit thought. *I've been drugged.* The knowledge made her understand why Amelia had looked at her like that. *I have to help her.*

"Who's depraved?" Branwen whispered, her face fiendish, flushed with passion. "Once, you flattened out at my command. You loved my depravity."

Twisting violently from side to side, Amelia shook her off, then stumbled to her knees.

The older woman accused, "You'd rather have Whitaker, now, wouldn't you? Well, she dies tonight, Kali, before your eyes."

"No," Amelia pleaded, "I'll do what you want. Don't hurt her. She has nothing to do with this."

Branwen swore. "I've had to watch her stalking you for weeks—that's reason enough. And *you*—you let her make love to you..." With two quick steps, Branwen closed in on Amelia, slapped her hard across the face.

Revived by a burst of anger, Whit's head cleared. *Make a plan*, she told herself.

"You belong to me, Kali. Say it."

No sound came from Amelia. She was crawling away from Branwen, toward the door that sealed in Maat's lab.

"I always felt so dark and powerful when I had you. You were my foil—so bright, so innocent, sweet."

Amelia's back was flat against the lab door and there was nowhere else to go. Whit distinctly heard her whimper when Branwen leaned down and gripped the front of the blue body suit. Branwen hoisted Amelia up, held her in place before her.

Do something, Whit's mind ordered. She got to her hands and knees and hovered there, the lethargy of her body receding like a tide that has reached the high water mark and turned.

"I won't open the door," Amelia said stubbornly.

Reaching into a trouser pocket, Branwen drew out a small palm computer. She pulled Amelia closer to the DNA plate. As Branwen touched the computer to the plate, the door slid open.

Amelia covered her mouth with her hands.

Indifferent, Branwen explained. "My reward for so often assisting Maat in her tiresome experiments. One afternoon, we successfully overrode the circuitry in a DNA plate. You see, I don't need you to open these doors." Branwen slipped the small unit back in her pocket.

Amelia protested, "It's not possible. I worked on the initial designs. It only accepts a live biological code...."

Branwen pulled Amelia inside the dark lab. From where she knelt, Whit could see them pausing by the steel door, the door that sealed the entrance to the underground vault.

"Touch the plate," Branwen urged. "It doesn't matter, now. The palm computer can open the door."

Peering at her, Amelia said, "If Mother knew the circuitry could be fooled, she would have designed a new plate."

Branwen gripped her, shook her. "Touch it!"

"It's my mother's code in that computer," Amelia guessed with a flash of insight. "*You* opened the Bordergate, *you* set her up before she could change the...."

Catching the wrist chains, Branwen tried to force Amelia's hand to the DNA plate on the stone wall.

"*No!*" Amelia gouged an elbow into Branwen's side and broke loose. Taking quick, unsteady steps out of the lab, she came back into the light of the hall.

Branwen straightened. "Get back here! For years now I've been trying to override this plate. There's a fifth barrier, a security back-up that Maat never told *any* of us about." Angry, Branwen came into the light. "Maat installed a force field on the *inside* of the vault. Every time I override the DNA plate, I trip that damned field!"

Amelia headed for Whit. "Get up," she called urgently. "Run. Please, Whit."

Striding closer, Branwen went on, her voice terse, "I had given up on ever getting beyond it. But there's one key left, isn't there, Kali? Your mother had such a habit of entering your DNA code in her security systems."

Amelia leaned over Whit, tugged her arm. Seeing Branwen advancing right behind Amelia, Whit stayed down.

With a rough shove, Branwen knocked them apart. Whit fell on her side.

Amelia whirled on Branwen. "Traitor! *Murderer!* My mother saw you for what you were, didn't she? In the end, she knew!"

Branwen smiled slightly. "After the mind-bond, no one believes any more that Maat betrayed Isis. It's only a matter of time until they start asking me questions.

"Don't you see it, yet?" Branwen gripped Amelia's elbow, speaking through clenched teeth. "I have nothing to lose any more. I'm leaving here with the codex. Every colony in Freeland will bargain with me for its safety."

Amelia fought to push Branwen's hands from her. A low, mean chuckle sprang from Branwen. She gripped Amelia by the hair and kissed her, obviously aroused by the resistance.

Something in Whit rose up like a quick storm on the Sound. She felt huge swells of rage washing through her legs, her arms. *Wait. There will only be one chance. Wait!*

Branwen coaxed, "Let's go open the vault." She began to pull Amelia back to the lab.

Crouching low, leaning away, Amelia made it difficult for Branwen to drag her.

"Cooperate, Kali. Or shall the Major pay the cost?" Branwen dropped Amelia and sauntered over to Whit.

With a cry, Amelia was up and hastily stumbling between them. She looked so upset, so exhausted. Whit's heart rose up and leapt out to her.

Branwen laughed. "Our Major is gifted in the art of passion, don't you think? Such an intoxicating lover. I never ruled her as I ruled you. She would not allow it. There is still so much for her to learn about pain and pleasure."

As Branwen reached for Whit, Amelia hurled herself, shoulder-down, into the woman. They rolled away. Amelia scrambled up and into a fighting stance. Branwen rose laughing.

She kicked out twice. Amelia dodged clear, then tripped on the ankle chains and went down.

Whit concentrated on silent stealth, and unsteadily got to her feet and made herself balance.

They were wrestling on the granite floor. Branwen was on top of Amelia, using the shackles to their best advantage. Steadily, Branwen was pressing the wrist chain closer and closer to Amelia's throat. Amelia's arms gave out. The chain came down, pressed into flesh. Amelia was wheezing, then gagging. Then even that was abruptly gone.

Whit became a precision machine.

She focused all her drunken faculties on getting the choke-hold right. She bent, locked her arms on either side of Branwen's neck. She squeezed and arched back, lifting the woman clear of Amelia. Branwen clutched frantically at her neck, then dangled limp.

True to her training, Whit held her there, feet off the ground. And Branwen came to life again, ending the ruse. She yanked a dagger from a sheath on her belt, jabbing blindly backwards. Whit felt the blade graze her leg, felt a jolt of pain. In response, she squeezed her arms together, a human vice.

She had no idea how long she held the woman there like that. Time was bent by the drug in her veins. Gradually, she knew that Lilith was beside her, telling her to put Branwen down, telling her that it was over. Lilith had to help her straighten her arms and release the woman.

When Whit loosened her grip, Branwen fell like a rag doll, her head at a weird angle. Whit looked around for Amelia and saw Styx gathering her from the floor. She cradled the shining, corn-colored hair against her shoulder, giving Whit an approving wink. Then Styx was carrying Amelia, saying, "Let's get them both to Cimbri, quickly."

Kneeling, Lilith checked Branwen. She felt for a pulse, then seemed to give up the effort. Lilith plucked a bandanna from Branwen's pocket and tied it around Whit's thigh. For the first time, Whit noticed the small red pool at her feet.

Whit felt herself staggering from side to side as Lilith steered her toward the door. She began humming again, trying to keep her mind occupied, her legs moving.

"Don't faint, Whit," Lilith said softly. "You're too big for me to carry."

Whit broke off her little song and nodded gravely.

They passed through the Council Room. At first, Whit thought it was Amelia standing there, then saw that the face was different. She stopped and peered at the strange, luminous being.

"Maat?" Whit asked.

Lilith had her arm, was dragging her forward. "There's no one else in here but us, Whit."

The golden-haired woman touched her fingers to her lips, then gestured toward her. A kiss. She was being given a kiss.

"Don't choo shee her? Sheesh dere," Whit said. "Sheesh pretty, like Amelia...like Kali."

Lilith turned and followed Whit's gaze.

Whit heard the voice tickle in her ear. She repeated to Lilith, "She says thank you for helping with the Bean Sprout. And marry Styx." Whit guffawed softly, amused by the nonsense of it.

Lilith grew wide-eyed. She turned a hard look on the area Whit had indicated.

The glowing woman evaporated. Whit waved and set off for the hallway, reeling from one step to the next.

Lilith hurried to keep up with her, glancing over her shoulder in wonder.

There was a noise like the surf coming in on a stormy night. How could she hear the ocean in the mountains? Whit passed through the door of the Cedar House and realized it was voices she heard—women's voices. They were cheering, hundreds of women gathered there in the meadow, cheering.

Then she noticed the ships. Great and small vessels of light hung suspended in the night sky, the bright mountain stars dimmed by the search beams that swung this way and that.

It seemed that all of Artemis had come looking for them.

*****

Kali leaned over Whit's sleeping form, gently tugging a comb through knots of dark hair. Her eyes were burning with fatigue, her whole body ached with the long battle the last 24 hours had been. Yet, she couldn't leave Cimbri's clinic without doing this. Lilith and Styx had tried to argue her out of it, but Cimbri had just brought her a comb.

Cimbri understood. Nakotah was still near death in the life-support chamber across the hall.

Setting the comb aside, Kali pushed her fingers between the strands, down to the scalp. The dark eyelashes fluttered, then slowly lifted. Kali gazed into the smoke-colored eyes and watched comprehension seep into Whit.

"Oh Mother," Whit cried. "I killed Branwen!"

Kali slipped into the narrow bed and held her. After a while the sobs slowly shifted into sniffling, and then into the gentle breathing of sleep. By that time, Kali couldn't bring herself to disengage from the rock-solid feel of her.

Cimbri and Lilith returned to find them asleep in each other's arms. Lilith remarked that they couldn't be comfortable like that in such a narrow, little cot. Cimbri promptly took Lilith by the sleeve, escorted her out to the hall and told Styx to take care of her. Nodding shrewdly, Styx led Lilith away.

Then Cimbri went to the life-support unit and watched over Nakotah. She stood there, studying the chiseled features of that face, praying for a future she hadn't known she wanted, until Nakotah had waved it before her like some glorious carrot.

*****

They were at the top of the hill, overlooking the ruin of Isis, exposed to the wind and rain. The other graves in the cemetery were lower than this one, farther away. A Leader rested here, alone.

Whit squinted against the fine drizzle of rain, watching Kali. The handful of flowers were scattered on the circle of stones that marked Maat's grave. The tears no one had shed for Maat were being shed, now.

"Do you see her?" Kali asked Whit hopefully, the voice still slightly hoarse from the choking she had been given over two weeks ago.

Whit shook her head.

"I don't see her any more, either."

Whit heard the sadness, the disappointment in her. "If you saw Maat again, what would you do?" Whit asked, knowing the answer.

"Tell her I love her, I miss her. Tell her...I'm sorry."

Whit slipped an arm around the wet warrior's jacket. "I think your mother knows that," Whit said gently.

Kali turned into her arms and whispered, "I love you."

They stayed there in the rain a long time.

*****

"...I never said I saw a ghost," Whit qualified.

They were gathered in Lilith's main chamber to celebrate the Winter Solstice. The room was lit by lamplight at four in the afternoon, as the sun coming through the huge window was now at it's weakest strength of the year.

Whit slouched in a high-backed shaker chair with a boot on one knee. Lilith and Styx were parked in the loveseat nearby, holding hands. Cimbri was pouring hot brew into a cup and passing it to Nakotah, who lay on the couch beneath blankets. "Well, then, what was it?" Lilith demanded.

Whit shrugged, shifted uncomfortably in her chair. "A lady who looked a lot like Kali," she replied.

Lilith raised her eyebrows. "A lady you saw and I didn't."

Cimbri said teasingly, "Whit had about six more hours of sedation drug in her. We're lucky she didn't see Sasquatch."

Nakotah tossed a pillow at Cimbri. "Don't mock my brother of the forest."

Cimbri hurled the pillow back.

"If you spill brew on this rug again...." Styx began.

"You're not allowed to threaten me," Nakotah informed her. "I'm still convalescing."

Styx, Lilith and Whit laughed.

Cimbri sent Nakotah a frown. "Leave the pillows alone," she instructed in a low voice. "You still need to conserve your strength."

Nakotah smiled, basking in the attention. She leaned back into the sofa and Cimbri readjusted the blankets. As Cimbri moved away, Nakotah caught her hand, and Cimbri sank down on the floor near her.

Lilith noticed Whit watching them, the gray eyes dreamy, the hands draped over the edges of the armrests, utterly relaxed. Lilith asked, "How is life with Kali?"

Whit returned, "Good." The shy grin that followed said so much more.

Lilith reached out and patted Whit's shoulder. "In truth, I've never seen you looking like this."

"Like what?" Whit laughed, self-conscious.

"Like you've been well exercised," Nakotah remarked. Cimbri promptly pinched her and Nakotah squawked.

"Like you've discovered the road to inner peace," Styx pronounced.

"We all seem to have found that road," Lilith said.

"It's not a road, it's a woman," Cimbri stated.

"The lover as conduit—yes—" Nakotah began.

Cimbri cut off the banter with another pinch. Nakotah retaliated with a tickle-attack. Cimbri rolled away with a howl. Nakotah threw off the blankets and dove onto the floor, pinning Cimbri beneath her.

Kali came strolling through the chamber door. "Nakotah is still weak, I see," she remarked above the noise. Kali went to Whit, kissed her and sat down between Whit's knees. Whit leaned forward in the chair and hugged her.

"She's driving me crazy!" Cimbri stated, pushing Nakotah off of her. "I long for those days when she was quiet in bed...."

Nakotah interrupted, "I have never in my life been quiet in bed."

"Yes," Kali interjected. "In the barracks her snores are legendary."

Nakotah shouted over the laughter, "Have you re-joined us, then?"

Kali nodded. "As a reservist, like Whit. It took all afternoon to straighten out the computer files. They had me listed as a deserter."

The room went quiet. Whit leaned over and grabbed Kali, murmuring, "You're under arrest." Kali blushed scarlet and giggled.

"None of that, none of that," Cimbri declared. "You're here to socialize with us, not each other. Save that for the long, rainy winter when you're house-bound on that farm."

Styx inquired, "What's this I hear about the two of you being nominated to stand for Leader next year, after Lil retires? Won't that interfere with your country life?"

Kali and Whit looked at each other. "You tell them," Kali said.

"We're both declining nomination," Whit announced.

"But why?" Lilith asked, incredulous.

"We think Cimbri and Nakotah ought to stand for Leader in Artemis and jointly share the job," Whit said soberly. "The duties of colony Leader have become too wearing and all-consuming for one woman. Cimbri and Nakotah are both just and well-respected. The urban-growth plan they submitted to the Council last week demonstrates how well they work together."

The other women looked around at one another, agreeing, yet puzzled by this news.

Styx narrowed her eyes. "And what will you and Kali be doing?"

Kali met her gaze. "We want to re-settle Isis."

Lilith murmured, "From the ashes, like the Phoenix."

Whit continued. "I'm donating my farm to the Agri-Science Center. They're going to use it as a field-study station. I'm going back to my mother's property in the mountain valley. Kali and I will re-build the house and barn, get the land ready for spring planting, and then live there while Kali pursues her own work."

Lilith surveyed Kali. "And what work is that, Bean Sprout?"

Kali grinned sheepishly. "There are many unfinished projects in my mother's lab."

Lilith beamed. "As Maat always said, a born scientist."

Nakotah remarked, "A born warrior, too. A strong woman performs well in more than one career."

Cimbri commented, "You sound like a politician, already."

Nakotah grasped Cimbri's shoulders. "I'll have many edicts concerning you, my pretty."

"Oooh, this could be fun," Cimbri laughed.

Lilith shook her head at them. "You have to get elected first. Despite your recent successes, your reputations are simply awful. Years of womanizing, selfishness, lack of direction. You would have had no chance for political office in my day."

Styx asked, "Was this the day of that crazy flyer, the one who tested the first methanol-powered jetcrafts? The one who bedded that mechanic on the blueprint table and came to the test flight with ink stains all over her jumpsuit?"

Nakotah whooped her approval. Lilith hid her face behind a hand and they all roared with laughter.

Shortly afterward, the group moved downstairs to make the Solstice meal together.

Kali and Whit lingered in the room, standing by the window, watching the day's end. The silver waters of the Sound glimmered with the orange and pinks of a weak December sun. They held one another, mesmerized.

Two strong-winged Canadian geese suddenly appeared, winging their way out to the water. Through the window glass they could hear the forlorn honking cry.

"They're partners," Kali said softly.

"Like us," Whit agreed.

They grinned at each other's foolishness.

"What are they saying?" Kali asked.

"'Welcome home, Kali. Welcome home.'" And then Whit gave her an earthquake of a kiss.

Far away, they could hear their friends shouting with laughter, waiting for them to share a meal.

The End

Biographical Sketch: Jean Stewart

Jean Stewart was born and raised in the suburbs of Philadelphia. She grew up loving any and all sports, enthralled with nature and music. She spent years trying to achieve her childhood dream of reading every book in the Swarthmore library, and is now afflicted with a voracious appetite for books.

She has taught school, coached hockey, lacrosse, and basketball, driven a truck and supervised railroad freight—all while writing books in her head. She is currently working on another novel, the sequel to *Return to Isis*.

She lives near Seattle, in the splendor of the Pacific Northwest, with her life-partner, Susie.

It is her heart's desire to live long enough to see a woman elected President of the United States.

If You Liked This Book...

Authors seldom get to hear what readers like about their work. If you enjoyed this novel, **Return to Isis**, why not let the author know? We are sure she would be delighted to get your feedback. Simply write the author:

Jean Stewart
c/o Rising Tide Press
5 Kivy Street
Huntington Station, NY 11746

RISING TIDE PRESS

OUR PUBLISHING PHILOSOPHY

Rising Tide Press is a Lesbian-owned and operated publishing company committed to publishing books for, by and about Lesbians, and their lives. We are not only committed to readers, but also to Lesbian writers who need nurturing and support, whether or not their manuscripts are accepted for publication. Through quality writing, the press aims to entertain, educate, and empower readers, whether they are women-loving-women or heterosexual. It is our intention to promote Lesbian culture, community, and civil rights, nationwide, through the printed word.

In addition, RTP will seek to provide readers with images of Lesbians aspiring to be more than their prescribed roles dictate. The novels selected for publication will aim to portray women from all walks of life, (regardless of class, ethnicity, religion or race), women who are strong, not just victims, women who can and do aspire to become more, and not just settle, women who will fight injustice with courage. Hopefully, our novels will provide new ideas for creating change, in a heterosexist and homophobic society. Finally, we hope our books will encourage Lesbians to respect and love themselves more, and at the same time, convey this love and respect of self to the society at large. It is our belief that this philosophy can best be actualized through fine writing that entertains, as well as educates the reader. Books, even Lesbian books, can be fun, as well as liberating.

If you share our vision of a better Lesbian future, and would like to become a part of a network helping to promote these publishing goals, please consider making a contribution, any amount appreciated, to Rising Tide Press, so that we may continue this important work into the future.

Other Books From Rising Tide Press

YOU LIGHT THE FIRE

Kristen Garrett

Here's a grown-up *Rubyfruit Jungle*— sexy, spicy, and side-splittingly funny. This humorous, erotic, and unpredictable love story will keep you laughing, panting with lust, and eagerly waiting to see what curves the author tosses in your direction. Kristen Garrett, a fresh new voice in lesbian fiction, has created two unforgettable and lovable characters in Mindy Sue Brinson and Cheerio (yes, Cheerio) Monroe. Can a gorgeous, sexy, high school math teacher and a raunchy, commitment-shy ex-rock singer, make it, and make it last, in mainstream USA? They will capture your heart and your imagination.

$8.95   **ISBN 0-9628938-5-4**

****

FACES OF LOVE

Sharon Gilligan

A wise and sensitive novel which takes us into the lives of Maggie, Karen, Cory, and their community of friends. Maggie Halloran, a prominent women's rights advocate, and Karen Weston, a brilliant attorney, have been together for 10 years in a relationship full of love and conflict. When Maggie's heart is captured by the young and beautiful Cory, she must take stock of her life and make some difficult decisions.

Set against the backdrop of Madison, Wisconsin, the characters in this engaging novel are bright, involved, '90's women dealing with universal issues of love, commitment and friendship.

$8.95   **ISBN 09628938-4-6**

More Books from Rising Tide Press

ROMANCING THE DREAM
Heidi Johanna

Author and journalist, H.H. Johanna, makes her debut as a novelist with **Romancing the Dream**—a captivating and erotic love story—with an unusual twist.

This imaginative tale begins when Jacqui St. John leaves northern California looking for a new home, and cruises into the seemingly ordinary town of Kulshan. Seeing the lilac bushes blooming along the roadside, she suddenly remembers the recurring dream that has been tantalizing her for months—a dream of a house full of women, radiating warmth and welcome, and of one special woman dressed in silk and leather.

But why has Jacqui, like so many other women been drawn to this town? The answer is simple, but startling—the women plan to take control of this little Oregon town and make it a haven for Lesbians.

$8.95   ISBN 0-9628938-0-3

****

EDGE OF PASSION
Shelley Smith

From the moment Angela saw Mickey sitting at the end of the smoky bar at the Blue Moon Cafe, she was consumed with desire for this cool and sophisticated woman, and determined to have her...at any cost.

Set against the backdrop of colorful Provincetown, this sizzling novel will draw you into the all-consuming love affair between an older and younger woman, and will keep you breathless until the last page.

$8.95   ISBN 0-9628938-1-1

ORDERING INFORMATION

These books are available at your local feminist or Lesbian/gay bookstore, or directly from **Rising Tide Press**. Orders under $25, send check or money order. Orders **over $25** may also be charged to Visa/MC using our **Toll-Free** number: **1-800-648-5333**. If mailing charge orders in, please include account number, expiration date, signature. Charge orders shipped in 48 hours. All mail-in orders please include **$4.50** for shipping & handling. Send check or money order in U.S. funds to **Rising Tide Press, 5 Kivy St., Huntington Station, NY 11746**

WRITERS WANTED!!!

Rising Tide Press, Publisher of Lesbian Novels, is Soliciting Quality Fiction Manuscripts

Rising Tide Press is interested in publishing quality Lesbian fiction: romance, mystery, and science-fiction/fantasy. Non-fiction is also welcome, but please, no poetry or short stories.

Please send us the following:

- One page synopsis of plot
- The manuscript
- A brief autobiographical sketch
- Large manila envelope with sufficient return postage

RISING
TIDE
PRESS

5 KIVY ST.,
HUNTINGTON STATION,
N.Y. 11746